WHAT LINE?

TAVISHA SH.

PAJDHASHI

hope

infinity will reunite with eternity

forever

intertwined endlessly

Poet's First Words

Born to a world

That can be home for the wild girl

For the natural knowing, life is part of a soul's divine
trace

In the mirror, we each meet her face-to-face

And in the same feral skies, we whirled

As the flames we carry unfurl

DECREE

Imagine an area of land home to a flower and a tree. Both as alive as can be.

Tree looks at Flower and says through a sigh, "You are too delicate in existence, not as mighty as I, the tree."

Flower looks at Tree to reply, "You are too loud in your presence, not as humble as I, the beauty." The two friends laugh over these bickering moments for they are aware of a balance in nature; not everyone is you and to impose your truths can be a sin you see.

One day, a bee stops by Flower with words that bring alarm, "Flower! Flower! You must be careful, there are these sleeping animals who walk on two feet coming this way! Today! They seek a beauty unlike another. Flower! Flower! You must hide yourself. Do not let them see your beauty for it shall be the end of you and Tree."

Having heard their trustworthy friend's warning, Tree starts panicking, "What do you mean the end of Flower and me? No, this will not do. I shall bear fruit from me so that these passers let us be." With the help of their Mother, Tree produces fruit from growing branches. When the animals on two come 'round, they lay no eye on little Flower near the ground. Instead, they pick the fruit from the mighty Tree and go on their way it seems; leaving Tree and Flower safe and sound.

However, relief felt by nature lasts merely a moment. The animals soon return with many more in tow. Dripping with greed and envy of their friends, they take all there is to receive until one shout, "There is no more!!"

The end?

With this apparent end, they go on their way, leaving Tree and Flower to enjoy their day. But the animals are not yet done; their conquest of nature has only just begun. They return yet again with tools in hand. They take from Tree all that can be given, from graceful leaves to steadied branches while a helpless Flower begs, "Please, take me instead!"

They take, and take, and take, until a stump is what remains. When they leave, Flower cries, "Dear friend, I am sorry. To protect me, you have been torn apart Tree."

"Don't cry dear Flower, I am still me, mighty as I can be."

"At least now, we can be together for eternity."

They stay together much longer, until a two-legged being presents himself yet again. "Well, what do we have here? A beauty we have spared?"

The animal cuts the blossom, leaving nothing but a stem bare.

Does our story end here? Having given everything to these humans? Now, Stump and Stem hope they can lay together endlessly.

Together, they sing songs about the pains that go on. Wind hears their song and passes it along. Earth knows its truth as it sows its roots. Water feels its sadness as it bears witness.

One day, another two-legged being comes along. This one had followed the song in the whispering breeze. It comes to our friends, old Flower and Tree, and weeps by their side for their spirits have survived.

Awaking from the sound of one of their children in need, Stem and Stump prompt, "Why do you weep for us child? We are as happy as we can be, for although we did not choose our story, we are free."

"How can you say that? Once mighty, once beauty, now empty?"

Stem and Stump abruptly find laughter yet again.

"Oh child, they have only taken some of what we are ready to give. Do not be so quick to see us dead when still alive and becoming. They can never take who we are nor who we can be."

"This is not fair; they took and took and took from you. All of you. How can you let this be?!"

"Child, we have been searching for thee. We have shared our songs with all of nature's creatures, but your kind's ears simply don't seem to hear. Your kind's hollow eyes only know how to hide. We have been waiting for you."

"For me? Why me?"

"We have been waiting for someone to help spread our decree. Someone with birthing fire inside."

And they remind their child, "Softness is not weakness expressed. Do not harden your eyes, do not encase your heart, do not impose your mind, and do not hide your soul for in doing so, you will forget us and render us obsolete. Do not forget, for even the gentle waters which trickle on your skin can turn sharp and carry your soul's shell off on a whim. Even the winds which dance with your hair can cause a whirl which steals your living breath. Even the earth which grounds your rhythm can tremble and swallow you in its core. Even the fire you need to keep you warm can turn you to dust in its sincere arms. When you don't respect our life, you don't respect your life. We do not say send these messages to scare you, but for you to understand that the true strength in our nature comes from our softness in being. We are not rigid; there is no resistance in our transformation. You, before all, must learn that softness is not weakness expressed."

Following this message, the child declares its gratitude for all the familiar beings it can name around. The spirits of life's expression listen patiently before revealing, "We do not need anything from you, not your gratitude nor your protection, not your wrath nor revelations, we have simply been waiting for you to enter our space. Dear one, we trust your kind's journey from innocent ignorance. You do not exist in a world in a trance. But we know the truth of your love, so we trust your journey. One day we will help you remember; we will help wake you from willful ignorance."

The child reluctantly feels the sadness only a baby seeking a refused guiding hand will remember. "Oh dear one, you have stepped through time, but try not to confuse our silence with absence. We do not expect anything of you other than you and because we know you, we will always love you. But, we are here to help you remember, we are all different expressions of the same essence that makes us, us. And before you ask what you are, remember that the question and fragmenting answers are already friends."

And with that came the beginning of this child's search for the smile nature softly carries in the strength that can never be swayed out of its tranquility.

Time knows and she shall show

It is easy to point a finger of blame
To maim the pain your shortcomings frame,
A manipulated picture of shame
To hide from your own defame.
Oh, I silently watch as your ego drowns your soul in
vain
For from your abandoned truth, you try to hide,
Still I see, he sees, she sees,
Even you in your treacherous decree can see
How the stains of sharp tongues
Have coloured your eyes blind and blind
And left the dust just untouched,
Where the absence of love,
You still clutch and unclutch.

Now a soggy feeling will sit inside you,
For your ignorance cannot have you saved
By the one you plead to; your crone on the throne,
The one whose mind you think is blank,
Unwittingly, the only one who knows who truly to
thank,
Not her blood bond, not her cloud bond,
Not her children spawned, wallowing in the slough
of despond,
But the ones living through love blazing,
Not haunted by delusions of 'we needed saving'.

Unlike you and you, sisters and misters alike,
Who clean four five times a day looking for light.
Preaching preaches not too loud that you can't
Hear your whispering misdeeds all around.

Oh, I hear your soft weep release since you can't
Proclaim that you only mislead because you grieve.
Insincerely hallow, no wonder a deceitful hollow
Is all you have found.

Oh well, some of us dream well and fine,
With peace and love and ample of signs,
And once again, don't think she's in decline,
Because she knows, oh she knows,
As she slows, as she grows,
Oh, she glows.
Mother knows Grandmother knows.
How do I know?

The divine whispers her heart's lines
And this time, I inked them from the sidelines.

But she reminds me,
how can we judge when we still don't know why
though we know that judgment ceases in the same
kingdom it is born in?
Something is happening in between.

.tavisha

BREAK IT ALL

The guards, farmers, merchants, mothers, daughters, sons, all the children, different but alike, stand in the grand clearing bordered by stunning jasmine blossoms. They should be joyfully awaiting the arrival of their daughter, but the air is paralyzed with angst for one of the men had received an invention that they had all been using in their leader's absence. They are eager to share the new toy with her, but weary and concerned for her reaction since the young woman had left them all in a delicate state. She is their protector but had needed to go away for a while to mend her bends.

Upon her arrival, the villagers all break out into dance. They wobble until the steady rhythm of the earth pulses through them.

"Let the festivities never end!" she proclaims. They all sing and dance as the Moon reaches its peak. When it meets its twinning point in the sky, a few women slowly gather on the sideline and eagerly make their way to their leader. Together, the audience cheers as they carry a veiled object as tall as their bodies and as near.

"What might this be?" she asks. The Sun reflects the gleam in their eyes as they let the veil fall and reveal what is hidden inside. In front of their leader stands a pool of water so clear that it reflects a perfect image back. Slowly, her face falls as she demands to know how many there are. Cautiously, the villagers reveal that they each possess one.

"It was a gift from a man who came while you were gone," says a brave one. They look at one another, none having expected this reaction. They had hoped the singing would last deep into the night, but now, they all know the festivities are over for even the jasmine cannot rid the air of the bitterness with which it is stained.

She looks in the mirror's eyes and in a trance-like state realizes; hidden between the lines, there are poetic rhymes. The mirror beckons her, "Hello old friend, are we going to forever pretend?"

She, blessed with beauty, life, passion burning endlessly. She, who does not let her power taint her mind. She, who thought, "I can leave all this behind."

She, who forgot her moment when. She, who sees in the mirror: life's end.

***

"It's been a fortnight now," the Elder whispers to her husband, "when is she going to speak again?"

"Who knows? Did you see the way she peered into the mirror? And it peering back? It has not done that before," he replies.

"There's another gathering tonight. We need to go to settle the others down to the cooling ground. They've been unnaturally disenchanted by the thought that darkness has pierced through her eyes and reached her soul—"

"Blasphemous words will not be uttered in my house!" he spits with a fierce glare that silences her, "We must not forget that this village raised that little girl and she is one of our own."

That evening, the villagers gather yet again. The usual air of praise permeates their time and space. The women's hair, decorated by the glow of blossoms shining brighter with the fading Sun, create a friendly reflection of the stars. Even though the humans dance merrily, it is unlike past celebrations when they would lose their mind and allow their swaying souls to move them. Tonight, their minds are alert and waiting. Upon their leader's usual arrival, they all gather in a circle. The villagers' hope was withering more and more each night for she had been giving her sermon in silence since her return. Tonight, she looks them each in the eye, resting on each one long enough to stir the light within them. The elder knows her eye and eye lock lingers a little too long and feels shame for the words she uttered before.

"Break them all! Break them all!! Burn it, shatter it, destroy it. All of it!"

"But why?"

"They've been stealing our soul!"

The villagers whisper to one another in alarm but do as they are told.

***

When the mirrors exist no more, she finds a temporary solace. Still, the memory of what she saw haunts her purest moments.

In the glassy eyes of a passerby, she sees painful truths that make her hide, "I am casting you all aside. Please, let me be. I do not want to see." She hides from all humans alike. She ventures out for walks in the night, hoping to play with the dying sparks. She finds a friend in nature as she wanders about. Under the Moon's watchful eye, she steps through the dark. She finds the river running by and in it discovers life's treasured why. She then begins hearing melodies hidden in the winds that blow and feeling the depth in the raindrops which appear to be shallow.

Now that she knows her '*why?*', she knows she can never hide. She knows that she can forever run from her reflection only if she can forever live in pretend.

The Moon wonders, 'Does she really understand?'

She walks as the thoughts she had suppressed start tumbling out. She fears their assault, but on, she walks.

Change is coming for me. The wind which caresses my skin will sweep the dirt and reveal what is buried underneath.

Still, she walks.

The ice was trying to stop the fire, but it will only make the waters rise higher.

Onward, she walks through the night to the day; through the dark to the light.

The sands are dry. They need the water to come to life; to show the hidden beauty and the darkness beneath sight. How do I fill the desert with water? How did it disappear? Is there too much earth and not enough water?

Too much ice and not enough fire? Or too much fire and not enough water? Is it because I stopped my tears from falling? From blossoming my memories?

She walks.

Earth that bore me. Fire that awakened me. Wind that soothed me. Water that nourished me. Help me. I can feel the music of the sea coming to life through me. I feel as though it can shake the ground I rest on and reveal the water. It's a madness that makes sense; a madness that feels like home.

As she steps on with the earth, the clouds join her, engulfing her and keeping her hidden in their protective embrace

They ask her where she is going but she doesn't know; she doesn't remember if she ran away but she knows she wants to go home.

They come together in front of her and allow her to step on with a silent welcome as though they've carried her before.

The cloud rises high but doesn't move towards where she ever intended to go. Still, she doesn't let the worry creep in too close for if she did, she would slip through the clouds and fall. Instead, she lets go and lets them carry her forward.

***

She walks until she runs into one of them again. The perfect crystal pool reminds her of her eyes, reflecting her true home.

"What is this?" she intentionally asks.

"I am sorry. We shall destroy this one now. It is the last and we were not too fast."

"No," she cries, "Do not act through wrath."

"Is this not what you ordered?"

"Yes, but this one is different, is it not?"

17

"I don't know what you see, but this is the very same one we unveiled for you," he speaks carefully. Perhaps the villagers and his wife were right, something was different within their beloved.

"Do you love the Moon?" she asks.

"I do not understand."

"Do you understand love? Look at the sky, do you not see both Moon and Sun above?"

"Yes. I see. The Moon is just like the mirrors we destroy; it steals the Sun's soul, passing it off as its own."

She gazed upon the sky.

"As I walked, I began to understand my fear's history and now, I finally see through the mysterious darkness. In there, I found a light that bends. We cannot break the mirror's core no matter how purposefully we try."

"But you were right. The mirrors have been taking the souls of the young; of our very Sun."

"Please understand. The Moon, without the Sun, is not able to shine and bring light to the skies, but the Sun alone cannot show the beauty of the unknown. The Mirrors of this world can never be destroyed nor need they be. You do not need to fear. None can steal a soul that has always been whole."

"Do come home with me and have some tea. We'd love to talk more about your journey." he requests.

"Of course, I'm beginning to realize how we all move towards wherever we are needed, no matter what it seems to be. Whether we feel lost or found, whether we feel we need to receive something or are the ones needed, it's all intricately woven."

***

At home, she sits with the Elder as her husband leaves them to prepare the tea. She feels the girl can see through her since she has finally unveiled her knowing of time. The young woman, feeling a wondering soul, peers and listens, but rather than becoming entirely frightened, she smiles as the strangest brilliance manifests in her eyes, almost like the divine itself is her even while they remain darkened.

Tea in hand, he returns to them with an unexpected question, "Why are your eyes sparkling my dear?"

"My eyes?" the Elder surprisingly asks.

"It's one of the powers," the girl says as she sips her tea, "to see the divine in another means to awaken to the divine in oneself."

"I know you may not want to share…or perhaps you aren't aware, but why did the mirrors frighten you so?" he inquires.

"Honestly, I felt both intrigued and betrayed by the mirror. They showed me what was hidden from me while erasing the memory. It leaves a quickly vanishing remnant of a soul. I don't know whose, but why give me love and then take it away?" she answers, quietly adding, "I was juggling my fear of a beginning and end. Is it worth it to start something that may end with an in-between that tears you apart? Honestly, I don't know, but something inside me keeps trying to remind me that love is the only thing worth it."

Someone gave me a special ring today
But I hide it on my wrist in sight
Clowning around like the truth I'm guarding
My soul only belongs with you

I love how you think death has a breath for me
As you worry if an unknown heart leans on my arm
If an unknown life has no charm
Don't worry, I can wash my bridge away
But then you'll have no choice to stay
And I know you hate how easily I am lead astray
                              Below the world's too grey
                                Above it's just a play
                              I chased the words you say
                              Shackled your pain away
                                I kept it from your day
                              But nighttime still remains
              I still love you on the other side of time
And I love how death has held his breath for you

                    And I know we've yet to talk
                  Though I learned your manners this way
                    Still don't know your face today
                  But I know the feeling of your eyes
                    Before I close mine in the dark
                    Hope it's enough for a spark
                      Hope love's a muse's fuse
                    Not just a reckless move

Because remnants of your mannerisms are seeping
into my days
Eyes glimpsing my way just long enough for me to
know
you're here to stay

.tavisha

Anastigmatic

Unfortunately prone due to a wiring they say
How I've grown tired of revising and rewriting their
play
Independence is a lie
I don't care if it's not on a spectrum's line
Independence is still a lie
At least when it comes to you and I

Impulsively neurotic, now enter a new dimension
Euphoric and free where I know you without a
mention
Moody and still dreamy without a mind for lost
intention
Pride and guilt now have flipped;
No more backdrops full of sins

They train children to be happy with a distance
All aboard, let's apply it to the world with scorn
If I could go home, I would without hesitation's
instance
Because here a tear is only free when it's controlled

How you feel means more to me than sincere
objectivity

Balancing a scale isn't where your soul's designed to
be
Pragmatic becomes problematic for a songbird's
poetry

.tavisha

DIA words

A shell momentously reminds the grain of sand
Dancing with a tormenting exclusion is not enough
to be forgotten
Rainbow pages travel without maps
Not knowing any notion of trust
Aware of outside hands opened to the sky in wait
Never grasped and still always innocent in their
playful reminiscence.

.tavisha

HOME

Imagine you are in a house. One that was built to protect you. There are sky high walls layered upon layers making a search for the core obsolete. These mazing walls were built for comfort; they always kept you warm. Some may even call it home. You are safe here. From within you can see through the barrier. You see the world for all its wonder, but you know all the torment that lays out there. You see the people stuck between two clouds, walking around carrying their storms inside, obscuring the true light of the sky.

One day, something comes knocking at your door. You wonder what's there for never before had something come forth. There have been whispers in the wind around, but nothing like this sound. It terrifies you, so you hide for a moment. Nonetheless, curiosity moves you towards the door and opens it a crack.

You take a peek outside and see love staring back. In shock, you slam the door shut. But you have already been exposed to its purity. As you fall before a closed door, you swiftly decide you will look once more. You slowly squeeze the door open and see love as sure as it can be. It starts to seep into the fractured entrance, but this door has protected you all your life, you've always chosen what comes and what goes without a fight.

Again, you close the door in fright. This dance keeps happening until one day the door slams open. You push and you cry as you try to close that open path to your soul. Boy, did you try. And love, feeling your disconnect, stayed out and allowed yourself to connect.

Door shut, you are safe yet again. Door shut. Sealed shut. Until one day again, you open the door. One moment again, you hope once more. You look outside and to your dismay, you cannot find love today. So, you close the door and go on travelling through your time within your restricting barricade. Safe and sound, you sing your song and dance your dance. Safe and sound. Until your heart starts to pound for none can go on this fragmented way; tearing your soul between love's embrace and fear's illusion of being safe. Your mind and heart confront you, demanding you choose between haunting memories of desires not yet known and daunting recluse in your veiled home. Abiding, you throw yourself to the door and hope love shows up once more. You hope. But tumbling your body against the walls, no matter how feeble, will never do, for you do not move through fear nor should you let it move through you. Still, you hope. Hope. Hope. Hope. Your hope never withers for your blooming mind is always becoming. And one day the walls start to fade away; dissipate into the sky. You look at this, as you start to cry.

These walls were built for comfort. They kept you warm. You thought this was home. Until they only caused you harm. Love made its way in and showed you the meaning of life. Showed you how to live again, how to feel alive.

As you look through yourself in this vast space, there are no doors to mark your home, no labyrinth to slither through.

What once was known is now no more.

Do you find yourself scared?

Looking in the air for doors to lead you?

Where?

Or will you finally realize that this love's vast unknown has always been your home? It has been waiting for a you who is not scared. A you who does not create prisons which are not there.

Wondering, haven't you been waiting for you too?

**My secret is I only jumped because I saw a rainbow
in the shadowed water and without knowing, I knew
the liquid gold waiting for me to meet its grace**

Do you see the rainbows bending to belong to your
tears?
Do you feel judgment's fears woven by your peers?
Do you know the trust you miss is yearning for you?
Do you see? Do you feel? Do you know?
Our skies are never only blue

Do you know
They're crying for you too?
They're falling for you too?
Waiting for you to come home too?
Craving you too?

Do your eyes catch the shadow's gleam or
Are they too blinded by light?
Because the night has folded itself into a crow
That calls for you
To bring you home
To a magic known.
Do you feel your shade of night falling into day?

Do you know
They're crying for you too?
They're falling for you too?
Waiting for you to come home too?
Craving you too?

Do you see the rainbows bend
just to belong to your tears?
Do you hear the star's swaying lullaby?
Way up high, can you feel?
Is any of this even real?
Oh, I don't know why I left that life of mine

But we always found love through our dreams
Even though the insidious art had me weak
And the river was drowning in my shedding leaves
Until I found your traces in my memory

You held my hand as we walked through the garden
of my mind
Carefully picking flowers left and right, not up and
down
We watched the glass tip away not towards us but
beyond time
I thought I was meant to stay unfound

But we always found love through our dreams
Even though the insidious art had me weak
And the river was drowning in my shedding leaves
Until I found your traces in my memory

Didn't you see the night fold into a raven just for
you?
Didn't you hear them calling from beyond?

Didn't you see the sun turning on and off
just to light your path home in pure gold?

All along the night was here
An echoing mask of fragmented fear
Surely this world has some place for me
Though I tried my best but couldn't adhere
To obstinately fixed memories
Of our history
Still shadowed in mystery.

But you always breathe
And you seep
Into my dreams
Where you win
Our circle's spin

. tavisha

here ; now

Remembering

"She always had this way of baring her soul
And then closing in too quickly
Leaving those exposed to such a rarity
In a state of awe that stilled their movement
All because she had been secretly seeking
fragments of lost memories

When I threatened to set fire to our past
She stood in the flames with her daring eyes
Knowing I could not try to let her die
Before carrying me back inside

And when I was dripping painful envy
I showed her a letter, a decree
See, you promised to never leave me
But she smiled at her lover's despair
At his thought that only a soul bond kept her there
And then she ran away, throwing herself into the
open air
Welcoming death without a care
Hoping one day it would lead to a love that stays
bare
Sacred and known before masks could be grown

But I ran to her and saw she was hanging off a cliff

Refusing to hold onto my hand anymore
Because she was trying to hold onto her soul
Turning, I heard her tell herself, "I'm sorry I was
wrong, I don't know if I can save you, but I love you"

Returning, I reached my hand out again but saw she
was still trying to save this soul
Even if it meant her end
She refused to let herself down
Until a cave opened itself to her

You should have seen her eyes
Miracles could have been born in them
As she gently placed her soul there

Desperate, she still refused my hand
Ignoring my requests for doors open
But her eyes were now smiling
Look, they said
Beside her, I saw a boy dangling
As a familiarity started growing in her eyes
Trust me and let go, they said

So, I did
I let go and fell into what she let me think was an
abyss

And too quick, her ground was there to catch me
As though she had risen herself to meet my skies
Never have I felt safer and she doesn't even know it
All because she closed her soul in too quickly"

.tavisha

Well, the circling's coming to its close
And I can finally see my home

I remember the fear of someone who claimed me as
their own
Upon my return after having gone around a circle
away from home
"Where have you been?" marked by a parent's
concerned control
And I, a confused child, clearly remember asking
and our exchange of "he can do it, so why can't I?"
"I thought you meant here, where I would always see
you. I didn't say you could move yourself out of my
way. What if something happened to you? How
would I know?"
But I was stubborn and insisted I had not strayed far
away
Although I remember the slight fear when I was at
my furthest from you
It merely quickened my pace on my return and
heightened my relief when I saw you waiting.

.tavisha

WRONG

A little girl skips around the majestic room, her eyes marking the rise and fall of every bounce. She has finally done it! She is 1 meter tall. She runs around excited, until her mom stops her and cautiously requests she stop beaming for her daughter could start entering realms she was too tall to be in.

"But…why Ma?" she asks, pleading with deep eyes of unwavering innocence. Venni looks at her and says with a heavy knowing,

"Some people don't like seeing others shining joy like a radiant sun because it reminds them that they aren't."

"But…when I'm happy, you become happy. And when you're sad, I am sad. Isn't it the same for everyone?" asks Avila.

"No, honey, you'll understand when you're older. Some things you don't share with other people."

"Isn't that lonely?"

"No, because you share them with the angels."

Avila looks at her mom, her eyes widening with excitement, "Angels??"

"Yes, they're always there if you need them for help or simply to talk, but they don't answer the way you and I speak. You must be able to listen to the voice of silence, then you'll hear. And remember, just because I told you to be careful with your mouth's smile doesn't mean you must control your eyes' spark. Now, lights off, it's time for sleep. Goodnight darling and sweet dreams."

This was the most open conversation this mother and child would have for the duration of Avila's childhood life. The other revelations would have to be shared in quiet whispers for the silencing of magic was still happening beneath the illusion of a harmonious reality.

****

"What do you mean 'I don't understand'? There is nothing not to understand. It's easy, just do it again!" her father yells.

"I want to go play instead. We aren't even learning this in school yet, why do I have to learn it today?"

"Fine, if you answer this question correctly, then you can go and play."

Avila hums a song as she tries to decipher the math in front of her, but still she cannot understand the answer. She tells her father a random number hoping he doesn't either.

"That's wrong," he sighs as she continues humming. "Stop singing and moving. You aren't focused. Don't you want to be smart? You're going to work on these problems until you can answer them all without doubt shaking your voice and blocking your mind," he barks.

She cries and begs, "Give me one more chance! Please!"

"Fine," he says. He didn't have the energy to argue with his daughter. His eyes were strained and sitting heavy in hollowness.

Avila moves through time, seeking to understand, not simply know. Looking at the equation, she turns it into a puzzle within her mind so that she can find the missing piece to make it whole. She also whispers to the angels, asking for help, but she knows not to tell anyone other than her mother who had warned her that she can't see through people yet. Her mother knows things others dismiss despite their curiosity. Venni had travelled from one side to the other, escaping the life she still leaves behind though she knows that it does not matter where one is, we cannot stray from our path. But for now, Avila is a child who wants to please, who needs others to believe in her for her to believe. As she looks at the problem, she beckons the answer to emerge. When she knows, she proudly tells him.

"Yes, that's right!! Ok, you can go play, but come back after to learn some more." Her father smiles to himself as she hurries off. He recognizes all the life in his little girl and hopes he does well, hopes she does well. He knows this is his duty, his responsibility, and he will succeed.

Avila does as she is told. Every time she gets the answer right, she's told to move on to the next one. After all, there are always new problems; new levels to attain. Every time she gets the answer wrong, she sees herself as a disappointment; a truth she imagines reflected in her parents' eyes.

***

Venni watches Avila's hopeful eyes which do not stray from her father as she grows. But Maro doesn't notice for he now often gets possessed by a sleep-living state. He won't recognize Avila's search for recognition under her optimistic pretense. Venni sighs as she goes back to drying the dishes. Maro used to tell her how strong Avila is; how nothing can phase her; how she is going to change the world. But most times, she fears that he doesn't even know her anymore. Venni often swallows words that surface. Words which would defend her daughter's wild, untamed mind. Words which would extend the horizons of Maro's temporarily well-kept mind. But

Venni often falls into silence, for she knows how cursed unwilling ears can be. The thoughts move up and down her spine as she thinks of her ancestors who had been burned before their time. She thinks of Avila, who already does not belong. *Maybe I made a mistake in telling her the truth,* she thinks. She glances up and notes the darkness marking a new moon. *I'll make this right and give my daughter the beginning she deserves,* she decides.

That night, with Avila in deep sleep, Venni enters her room. She warns the angels and guides not to interrupt her nor stop her from what she is to do, for her intentions are purely to protect her daughter from what the world has come to. *They never stop us anyway,* she thinks while reminding herself, *it's impossible to stray from one's path.*

Venni places one palm on Avila's forehead and another on her soul's center. She channels her energy and creates boundaries inside her. She sighs as she realizes that most people internalize other people's expectations and fears to create their own prisons inside, but Avila would not know the difference because of the blindfold she is placing over her eye. Venni knows that only that which moves with love can enter another, no matter the layers above so she creates a shielding envelope of darkness and reveals, "Now nothing will be able to reach you unless you reach for it first." Once she is done, she escapes her room as quiet as a shadow, leaving a deeply sleeping Avila under the moon's absent light.

A warning should have been shared this night that whenever one blocks the sight from another one's eye, they create a strong divide between their own soul's light and mind. It is the beginning of the fall into ignorance's enticing trance for all who witness shadows dance.

***

One day, Venni receives a call from Avila's teacher.

"I'm calling to speak about your daughter…" she says.

"Has something happened?" her mother asks.

"She did poorly on her test."

"My daughter?! But she's one of the best students in your class."

"Yes, I know. That is why I am calling you…I was wondering if anything has changed?"

"It's the same as it has always been. I don't understand how she could fail…even when she is ill, she always manages to succeed. She practices these problems every single day. Maybe you made a mistake?"

"I'll send the test home with her today and you can see for yourself."

Deni says, "Thank you," as she hangs up the phone. But her surface sweetness had already begun boiling into something sinister; no one was themselves anymore.

***

The young Avila goes home that day with an emptiness growing within her. She is terrified of what is to come. Venni drags her inside as she lets out her rage as though it has never been hidden away. The daughter sees it again; what she begins to believe is her mother's true face. A face that haunts her in her dreams. A face that was a rarity at first but had slowly merged into their normality. She feels the resentment in her voice, as though she had ruined her life. Her mother has mastered the art of taking her shame and turning it into blame. Venni, in these moments, pours envy, hate, anger, everything and anything into her daughter, then audaciously wonders why her daughter has a snapping temper. She didn't believe she was doing any wrong, after all, she warned her daughter when she was but 1 meter tall. She just never thought she would be the one to break her daughter's core.

But, Avila knows she can take it. She never had anyone to confide in and she wasn't eager to start trying. Instead she swallows the pain, thinking that's how you make it go away. Nevertheless, this pressured hole inside, it grows until it feels like an assault from within. Then, Avila explodes. Time and time again. She tries her best to hide it from them, to not add to the pain that they drown her in. Still, emotions are fickle and she is still a child; she hasn't yet learned how to control her laugh when she is tickled. But, Avila knows that she will never stop trying. She hears her mother tell her she's never ready and hopes one day she will be, but Venni hoards an unknown envy in her that she had to give up her gifts while her daughter was just beginning to know hers. She knows it isn't right to take out her frustrations on Avila, but she also knows she is temporarily only human. She hopes this may be a lesson Avila will need when she's older, though she knows she may just be taming her own guilty conscience. After all, you cannot force guilt on an innocent soul and so long as her mother kept doing so, her powers would not come back strong.

When Maro comes home, he takes one look at the score and doesn't speak to his daughter that day. Instead, he has her mother send her to her bed where Avila is filled with dread because she knows the masks are being shed. That night, the little girl goes to sleep as she weeps.

"She just needs to practice more," her mother tells her father. Venni knows that if the veils were shifting, then Avila would be acing everything. Something has blocked Avila and she can't help her. She knows that Avila has to go through this on her own and that she has to continue the play.

"Yes. She just needs to practice more, you're right," he echoes. This is the reality of her house. Echoes of pretense bounce off the walls until slowly they descend into echoes of silence.

The next day, their daughter goes to school as quiet as a mule. Her teacher worries that maybe she had overstepped. All she wants is for Avila to do her best. The little girl grows silent and although she also grows in silence, the light she shares dims itself, until is barely there. The teacher considers her reservations for a week before convincing herself that Avila has always been shy. It's easy to forget the memory of a person when it means one is safe from the flame; people can twist reality until they see people as they believe them to be. This is why it is better to be forgotten. Because then, you don't live on in people's memories. Avila isn't shy. She simply knows she must blend into the walls if she wants to survive. At least, for now.

Every night she waits for her verdict to be announced.

"Right. Right. Right. Right..." resonates all around.

Should there be a wrong, she'd have to suffer all alone.

***

Avila grows up conformed and contorted. She always aces her tests. One day, she grows tired. Tired of the chorus in her head. The one that sings her to sleep when she is right. The one that keeps her awake with shadows when she is wrong. She grows tired of fighting to always be right. She goes to school and decides it's time for her silence to fight. That day, Venni receives a call from the teacher again.

"Hello...I'm calling about your daughter."

"Yes, what happened?" Venni asks.

"She has failed her exam," the teacher announces.

"What…are you sure?"

"Yes…but…this isn't normal," her teacher hesitates but goes on to say, "she failed with a 0."

"How does someone get 0? I've heard it's harder to achieve 0 than 100. Did she not write the exam?" questions her mother.

"She wrote the exam and answered every question. She answered every single question…" Her teacher is as confused as her mother sounds.

"Her father and I will talk to her when she comes home to find out what's happened."

That afternoon when Avila walks through the gates, she wears the biggest smile on her face. Her father takes her and physically shakes her, "Why would you get 0 on an exam on purpose?!?! HOW IS THAT EVEN POSSIBLE?!" he demands with an aggressive groan.

"I don't care," Avila whispers, "I am done caring for your rights and wrongs." She goes into her house and runs to her room before she can feel her parents' madness.

"What do we do?" Venni asks. She thinks of all the late night talks she's had with Avila about the magic of this world. Her soul knows the world's truths, but her mind is clouded which is why she cannot remember. Maro, on the other hand, still knows none of it, and he wouldn't believe Venni if he knew the truth now. It would take a special person to be able to break through their veils which have grown as strong as steal.

"Don't worry, she'll come around," reassures her father.

Together, they fix her. Manipulation is the weapon of choice. Guilt and fear are the bullets of course. Avila is raised to be successful in the eyes of those around. She always knows to be right and not wrong; she always fights to be seen as right even when she knows she is wrong and thus, she finds herself all alone. She knows she has buried her light far away and wonders if the truth all along was she was never meant to play.

***

Her parents religiously wish her luck on her exams even though they know she always performs well. She is now well into University and will soon get her degree. Then, she will seamlessly become another part of this functional society. It is all going smoothly, until one day she finds herself faced with a bonus question during her exam.

Professor Lonso stares intently at his students as they write. He can almost feel the stress seeping from their bodies. He wonders why the educational system has become this way, but he knows that too many people need a hand to hold them no matter how old they get. He knows his students; he knows that without these exams, they wouldn't care to learn. The only reason they do right now is because of the system's deadlines. They postpone until they can't anymore. He worries that that they are postponing their lives away because they believe deadlines don't exist. But one does. Professor Lonso knows this because he is approaching his. He looks at his students and thinks, *"What would you, any of you, do if you were told that you only have a year to live? Chances are in favour of you starting to finally live. Why? Because you are now aware when your deadline is and it is a lot closer than anticipated. People will cram their lives in that one year. He's read plenty of articles which occasionally circulate about people's last words being filled with regret over not living. Their case is similar to a student who waits too long to start an assignment. A student who realizes that there is no point since there is no way they will be able to finish it in time. A student who feels they have no choice but to accept a failing grade. Do not wait too long. Do not build yourself a cage with fears you have internalized. Do not wait until you have no choice but to accept an unfulfilled life."*

Suddenly, he stands and moves towards the board as he says, "All of you need to perk up! Here is a bonus question for you all." He writes on the board as he says, "And here's a clue, stop being this". He sits back down while laughing.

"What colour is the sky?" she reads to herself. She wonders if it's a trap. She stares at this question for far too long until the edges bleed out and the words become blurred by her watering eyes for she doesn't know what to write.

She doesn't need to answer this given question, but she can't help but wonder. She experiences these moments of wonder often; when she allows her mind to finally wander. She has a strong hold on her mind, but sometimes the wonder seeps out the stitches she uses to keep her soul shut. Sometimes, she almost lets herself know that she sowed it imperfectly for this very reason; waiting for the moment it won't hold together anymore. Waiting. But life is not a waiting game. She knows the others will write down blue and leave quickly without a clue as to how this question phases her, but Avila can't move because she has a battle brewing inside her. She thinks she should do the same as the others and leave, but the thoughts in her mind condense like mist she can't see through. She knows what she should do. Instead, she writes what's going on inside her head.

"People may think of the sky as being blue, but it's not really blue. We see it as being blue because of the wavelengths and how the light is scattered. It's because of the way we see. Many have probably answered the question this way. Due to a given, limited perspective, people interpret the world while forgetting that perception is ambiguous in nature. It is meant to be ambiguous so that we do not falsely believe our interpretations to be the only truth. Furthermore, blue is the instinctive colour that came to their mind because they were taught to colour the sky blue. They were taught the word blue. They were taught what to believe is true. They can't be blamed; they're following a normality that was imposed to become their reality.

There are many colours the sky can be. It goes from white to black; from pink to purple; from cloudy to sunny and clear. The sky is not just blue; it is not just colour. It can be stormy and chaotic or calm and empty. It can be filled with stars or void of light. But some people only think of blue when they think of the sky. The people don't look to see all that the sky is and all it can be. Nonetheless, the sky is still all those things; much more than blue. Still, there's nothing the sky can do to stop people from thinking of it as they will.

People can be narrow minded, but the sky will not become only blue to fit what those people think or believe to be true."

***

Her response astounds Professor Lonso. *"This student is always so quiet yet has much in her mind,"* he reflects.

Avila stands in front of him tight-lipped, having received a request to meet at his office. He hands her a pamphlet and tells her that she needs to join this group of graduates who had formed a collective for people whose minds aren't bound shut. She tells him she will think about it, but he knows that she has made her decision from the look in her eye.

She knows this is not what has been seeking her.

***

"Hello, I am Professor Lonso from the university your daughter studies at," he impatiently states.

"Hello Professor Lonso. Do you wish to speak to her?" an aging Venni asks. Years of blindly

48

abiding to patterns of mindless behavior takes its toll on people.

"I actually want to speak with you and Avila," he says with an emphasis on the 'you' like her presence would have some influential importance. He does not know her daughter the way she does.

Her mother, although depleted and drained, energetically panics as she remembers the past conversations she's had with her daughter's teachers. "I think it would be best to speak to her father about this. He's the reason she has always done so well," she explains. Nonetheless, her professor requests that they both present themselves at his office the next day.

***

The daughter sits between her mother and father. They seem worried about what this professor will say, while Avila sits with a smile painted on for she knows that worry only exists when we live in anticipation of the future; another illusion of time.

"Your daughter is one of my best students. She always listens to understand. She always aces her exams...but...I want you to read this question and the answer right here," indicates the professor.

Her parents do as they are told as Avila waits quietly. She knows to obey even when she doesn't feel ok. When they finish reading, Professor Lonso asks them to share their thoughts.

"Well..." her father looks at Venni who says, "I simply don't know what to tell you."

"After reading this, I knew we had a special student with us. One who is wise and cares enough

49

to go further than necessary. I extended an offer to join this new collective, but Avila never made herself present." Professor Lonso knows he is pushing the limit, but the truth is that he had spent his whole career searching within him for a mind like Avila's, something only a seeker could understand. He wasn't going to let go of her now that he had her.

Her parents had their eyes glued to the books written by the collective. Their eyes were lighting up with something Avila had never seen. Flashes of pride, greed, and shame came over them the way she used to flicker the lights to see time shortened.

"Is there anything you have to say?" the professor asks the student.

"Is the answer right?" she slyly asks her father.

"I don't know, ask your professor," her father responds.

"Suddenly, you don't know what's right and what's wrong?" she pushes on.

"If you had just written something normal like all the other students, we wouldn't be in this situation today," he sternly tells her.

Professor Lonso looks on with amazement. He wonders why her parents don't realize the brilliance they were trying to shatter. Meanwhile, Avila is seething. All her life, she tried to calm the fire that was growing within. Instead, she continually found herself quivering. She doesn't want to fight nor to live in plight, she simply wants to feel her flight and all too swiftly, something breaks in her mind.

"THE SKY IS NOT JUST BLUE!" she yells as she deafens the room with her presence, "Why don't you take the time to see it as it really is?!"

They all sit in shock. Her parents are frozen in embarrassment, no doubt already thinking of how to punish her. Her professor was feeling something different. Fear. Fear that he would lose the gold coin he had only just found. He opens his mouth to appease the situation, but that predictable and intended interruption is enough to set Avila off again.

"And. You. You only want me for some ulterior motive and I don't care to stay around trying to understand what that is. I do not care anymore. You are just as bad as them. You put me in a box labeled intelligent and didn't bother to learn my name until what? Until I told you that blue skies don't even exist. Recognize that NO ONE is just blue. No one! But no! People do not take the time. They notice the ones who are loud."

Avila pauses to breathe and lowers her voice as she continues, "Who notices the ones who are quiet? Who notices the sincere moments? Have you ever seen someone smiling as they read a poem? The smile is quick and it usually goes unnoticed. Do you ever get quiet because you're misunderstood? Do you ever gently hum along to life? Do you? Or do you really believe you are only blue? These moments that are expressions of who we are…who notices them? I'm tired of the hypocrisy of this world. I notice for my sake. You should become aware for your sake!"

The air in the office is vibrating with tension. Avila gets up and leaves, but not before telling her professor, "You are searching within minds for something that does not lie there. Not in theirs, not in yours, and not in mine. These students of yours conform because they don't mind a temporarily controlled in-between, not because they don't care helplessly, though you'll only know this when your sweetly veiled hope has died and sends you into your abyss to find what still can thrive, what was always alive. And what, after death, still lives."

It is another 5 minutes before the Professor clears his throat and blinks his eyes in confusion. Her parents shake their head softly as if they had been in a trance. Without a word, they leave. There is a change in both of them. They move through the world slowly as if the air is as thick as water. They make it all the way home in silence where they find an envelope with a letter inside. The letter is started by the heart of an unknown soul. It says,

'Dear Angels, I'm sorry, I know you want me to dream but I don't know if I am allowed."

and is continued by a child's hand,

"Dear Angels, in my house, everything is imaginary. Things are better, I can see the light in them, but it dims as quickly as it is ignited. I don't know when I will be free to follow my dream."

and is finished by an adult grown,

"In my house, everything was thrown indirectly. The hush words spoken softly, barely a whisper that I could hear audibly. They told me the things I felt, heard, and saw... the things I lived were imaginary. Well, my sad reality is that both words of

love and hate were whispered almost silently. They were planted in all of us and the food the world around me used to nourish them was fear, anger, jealousy, sorrow, and pain. But that wasn't enough. They came for me. I heard the thoughts in their head. "We don't like your light…we don't like that you're happy…let's make a trade…I'll spend time with you…so you won't be lonely…I'll be your friend…but I'll trade my darkness for your light…again and again." I wish I could silence them. The voices on repeat in their heads. But I always had a home. Or so I thought. Until the whispers of love became absolute silence and the whispers of indifference grew into roars and violence. But I always told the sky I could handle it. I always had angels with me; I believed you when you told me that they would always protect me. My light has grown more and more. When I was 8, I promised my angels I would stay only until it pierces through your dark. Today, I made another promise that I would stay with people until their darkness goes away and they told me I am endless light whether or not I keep sharing it. When Professor Lonso called me wise, I knew then. I knew that the wisdom he was referring to is the shadow my pain casts and though these shadows are now my dear friends, I also know that the shadows cast can also be shadows of light. I refuse to stand by those who eagerly stitch the scarlet letter on someone's hand because of their need to look down to look up. Whether roles are reversed or not, the division is what caused the drought, so now, it's my turn to disappear and no one will bring me home but me."

With those last words, both Venni and Maro knew that Avila would not be found by them.

***

She chooses to live her truths instead of walking around pretending to be dead. That night, as she sits on an empty park bench, she hears the voice of silence again. It sings to her and reveals that it had never left her. She had simply buried her gifts too deep for her to able to hear them. But, they were always with her, waiting patiently for her to unbury the ocean beneath the ice. She cries as she listens to the song she thought was long gone. She makes a vow with the tree in front of her to always carry that song even when she feels alone.

***

Venni, to this day, turns that weathered down paper in her deeply engraved hands. She holds it tight the way she used to crush Avila against her skin. It has been struck by time, but the heaviness it once held has slipped away. The clasp on her throat and heart, when she had first read the words through the blur of her tears, had then immediately begun its release. Her daughter had unknowingly liberated her from feeling pain solely in the front of her body and had given her the strength to stretch her spine out and raise her head high.

She instinctively turns her chin when she hears the usual thud of Maro's march, but her eyes remain fixed on the letter. He greets Venni with a kiss on her forehead and eager eyes. He notices the

54

letter folded in her hands and asks, "Do you remember the day she left?"

"How can a mother ever forget?" Venni says laughing, "The first thing a mother finds when a lost child returns home is relief from a grief that never would have healed."

"I can't believe you tried to keep her magic a secret from me, let alone her!" The air was lighter in the manor. It had been ever since Avila had awoken again. "Well, you know that everything turns out perfectly…as usual."

Maro furrows his eyebrows as he tells her, "Well, you, my dear, may have known, but we were riddled with doubt as to whether she would succeed."

"We? As in the angels? Liar, you don't feel doubt."

"We are also not allowed to do many things I've done," he reveals, "Perhaps the rules of my universe work differently now. Ever since Avila's arrival, things have surely changed."

"All I can say is that it is a relief to have you awake and no longer asleep." Venni says as she shivers at the memories of his eyes when she knew they were comatose; at all the times she wondered if this was their punishment for the life they chose. But, there was always a purpose and always meaning, she had known this since she was young. Every moment lived is not a casual coincidence but a moment of synchronicity. It simply is that humans abide by the rules of time differently and do not realize the connectivity.

"Do you think she knows?" Venni asks Maro.

"Perhaps. We never could tell her, but you know how she listens to that precious silence of hers. It probably told her everything. Now, it's up to her to remember. She always had that persistence, even when quiet. She demands to be heard, to be seen, to be known. I'm telling you, she will change this world." They share a peaceful smile, knowing that they had done their part well even if Avila had not understood then and may have yet to understand.

***

"I have a surprise for you Venni," he says as he hands her a flower. This was a special flower that Avila had sent with her first letter home. It had been enclosed within the letter, marking its presence with its fragrance of heaven. In his hands, he holds a letter. "We've received another one!!" he says excitedly.

They open the letter and feel the overwhelming rush of the sea. They beam with happiness at what this means.

"Should we tell her to wait?" Maro asks the way only a protective father would.

"No, she won't live her life waiting," Venni responds the way only a knowing mother could.

56

A case?

A pencil?
When I think of a pencil...I think of what it's used
for...
It came from a living thing and from it we can
create many things
Even if we erase our creation, there's always a
trace that remains
Even if the trace is merely a shorter pencil,
~ what's the point of erasing anyways?
The pencil is not going to go back to its old self
whether you erase or not
Because it gave part of itself and you used it
What was it used for?
Did you just write notes in class? did you doodle?
or scribble?
Did you write a story? or a poem? or a song?
Did you draw? Or?
Did you write math comparisons you barely
understand anymore?
You chose what to do with that pencil ~~~
And with each stroke that pencil disappeared to
become what you made of it
What did you use it for?
Something you love? or something you hate?
Something you're bored of?

Because that pencil no longer exists
All that remains is what you create

~~~~~~

here ; now

What about a paper?
It's blank and eager,
excited for the
stories or messages
secrets or drawings
it might carry near,
but what if the paper feels
like you're staining it with
what you choose to do,
giving it a story it never
asked for,
poor paper,
quietly hoping the person
will create something it
sincerely wants to wear

.tavisha
~~~~~~

Man,

whose attempts to steal hidden glimpses
have always turned up empty,
will become bitter and express resentment
in the face of beauty.
Should the presence make itself absent,
only then will the choice be made to either feign
indifference or to embrace existence
once again.

Presence is known in absence
just as absence is known in presence.
For those awake in their ignorance
will never sleep peacefully
neither in day nor in night,
but rather dream haunting memories of the light.
                    .tavisha

Stagnation

The blindfold hath been placed
By i and i's embrace,
My memories all erased,
Even of my face.

On and on i went,
Not knowing what i meant,
Until one who knows no bound,
Knows no distance can be found,
Until one remains
Who knows these things which flow through
cannot be explained,
Marking chaos' hurricanes blending 'i's separated
into I
Back together again.

But sometimes two fall apart in a dance
To spin in on themselves before coming back
together,
Mirroring each other,
Blending into one as the dissolution itself ends.

We don't seek an orchestrated love,
We don't want to fall into a safe game of pretend,
So, unless you can see through shadows,
You won't find our soul hiding in the hallows.

Then comes the moment soon,

When one can still oneself long enough
While looking at the transparent water
That a reflection emerges before falling in again,
And as one falls in,
Like a drop that saw itself reflected in the ocean,
'one' ceases to exist
And then, even sooner,
The game of distance in space and time concludes
and no witness is needed for what unfolds.

.tavisha

here ; now

ONE DAY

Every day, the young man walks by his neighbour; an elderly woman who would never harm a tree. Every day the young man gets angry. He would get angry because he did not find it fair that she had more happiness than he. Every day he wonders. Every day he ponders. One day he asks her, "Why do you act so happy and free?"

"I do not act, I am. I'm not putting on a show of pretense for your eyes to see."

"You are what then?"

"'I am' is enough, 'I am' is all I can be."

He continues on his way, confused from what the old lady has to say.

Every day he seeks answers; he needs to know why. He seeks from the books in the library to the presence in the sky. One day he tells her, "You make no sense." That day he walks quickly, not ready to repent.

One day his neighbour is not there. That day his parents tells him she'd been fighting for air. Death has grazed her soul and soon her time will come to leave.

One day. One day. One day.

The man continues his usual way.

One day he sees his neighbour smile as he feels resentment arise again.

"How are you not drowning in despair when you know that death is near?" he demands.

"Ah, my temporary deadline is near, but I do not fear since it is not yet here. Don't you understand that it is in the knowing of my 'when' that I am set freer? I spend my moment, here and now, as alive as I am. You, on the other hand, young with life or so they say. You do not even know when it will be your day, yet you linger in anticipation for what's to come around. Not knowing has the potential to set you free but you're walking rigidly, tightly. So rather than waiting to meet your beginning's end, why not live your life right now instead?"

"How would you know anything about living life anymore, for years I've seen you sit with this tree of yours," he says with a pain almost bitter.

"It doesn't matter what I say, you'll understand it all on your one day," she adds before turning back to her mighty tree.

Here for infinity, now for eternity

They told me, "You'll go crazy in love."
But in love, I've forgotten what crazy means
And when they see me, they bask in my radiance and ask me
what my secret is,
"Become curious about love and remember yourself," is all I
could say,

I wonder if they'll hear me today.
Then, they ask who this love is for,
But I have no idea?
And then you ask how,
But when you ask how,
You are circling around what you already are

Anyways, it doesn't matter
All ways always lead to love
So any way, it doesn't matter
It is love's echo
The one that transforms you back into you: love

And now curiosity has walked you down a path,

Oh see, have you already forgotten?
Are you a walking paradox?
You're on one side of a gate, trying to get in,
Seeking the other side?
Look at how you tilt your head to hear something tell you the
key is love!

Something is happening, but in between is a blur,
But see!
That glimmer of love in your eyes is near
And now,
You're on the other side of the wait,
How coyly does your soul breathe a sigh of 'I'm here'
Then again, you still yourself
And listen to that same something ask "What gate?"
Whether you whip around or sneak up on yourself,
You know, there is no gate and you were never late.
"What key?"
"What paradox?"
"What there? What here?"
"What then? What now?"
"What love?"

.tavisha

I'm still mad at you for letting me believe in your nonexistence

That tree's page did not want to burn by the lake
Carrying wishes marked by an empty stay
I know it was your shadow kneeling beside me in yearn
But the ache that you might dissipate was enough to still my
moving hand from reaching for you in return
And it's absurd that I let myself believe your love was
something I had to earn

Were we bound to burn?
A trickster's guise with wide smiling eyes
You were right, they tried to set us on fire
Too little too late for swelling hearts with desires
When we know love is something that always burns higher

.tavisha

here ; now

MEMORIES
OF A LAKE

"Son, let me tell you a story. Come sit here comfortably.

There was once this man who wanted to go fishing, but he did not want to go just anywhere. He was desperate to go back to the lake where he had spent many of his childhood days. He carried memories of that lake wherever he went; every time he closed his eyes, he could see the spectacle of light where the air met the water. Son, if you can just imagine! It looked as though rainbow crystals were scattered all over.

He had all the equipment necessary but could never make the time to go. One day, he grew tired of his excuses. He went to the beautiful lake where the light shimmered and danced along the water's surface. It was not a perfect day to stay out for more than a few hours since the air was crisp and the water had already begun crystallizing. However, this man knew that if he did not go then, he would have to wait too long for his motivation to come alive again.

Then, just as he was about to push his boat out, he noticed a hole. He thought to himself that he would just deal with it later and off onto the water he went. As he set up his fishing rod, he noticed that the lake was seeping into the boat. He panicked and started scooping it out. While he was getting rid of the water, the fishing rod began to slip. The man stopped what he was doing and hurried to grab it before it disappeared to the bottom of the lake. He continued to scoop water out with one hand for a while until he realized that he wasn't removing enough. He wanted desperately to catch at least one fish that day and saw the sun setting which meant he would have to go home soon. So, he made a decision. He set the rod up on one side of the boat and went back to scooping the water out with both hands. The water started rushing in quicker and quicker. The man was caught in a cycle of removing water when he saw the rod shake. Son, that meant he had a catch, a rare pull from his dream! He knew that if he abandoned his current task, he would lose the boat, but that if he didn't, he would lose the rod and the fish."

The wrinkled man recounting this story takes a stretched pause, allowing his eyes to gallivant through his mind before continuing, "Some people would have never ventured out; would have never even known the hole that existed. Some people would have spent all their life preparing for possible holes and never knowing the feeling of floating. Some people wouldn't have noticed the hole until water started flowing in and some would have taken on a temporary ignorance like the man in the story. Some people would only become aware of the hole when they start to sink; some would only become aware when they start to drown. Some people would try to scoop the water out with clenched hands; some would try to use open hands. Both approaches wouldn't help in the end. Some people would be obsessed with the catch and let the boat drown, some would trust that they would make it back home somehow.

The man in this story went home without a fish that day. On his skin, the cool and light breeze was matched perfectly by the warmth of the sun. He laughed as he walked, dripping memories of the lake. He knew that he should not have gone fishing with a hole in his boat that day, but he also knew that his dream was meant to live no matter what he had to say."

He looks at his grandson, whose eyes are now blinking at a slower but steady pace. He looks to the sky which holds not a single cloud. It is bursting with colour which bleeds at the seams and blends perfectly to create a picturesque sight, one that no camera's eye has ever been able to grasp. "Time for bed, son," he says as he stands up and carries him off to bed.

He comes back out to the porch to find that the sun has already gone away, slowly realizing how quickly day fades into night. He sits on the swing which gives no sign of its age. He rocks for a moment then traces his palm, allowing his fingers to travel along the creases which are fading. He thinks of how these paths are fading from a life well-travelled; not untouched and dark like a path never known. He often stares into his hands, waiting for a dark crevice to reveal itself again. He knows he would not hesitate this time, for as quickly as a whale emerges from the ocean's depth, it can just as quickly submerge itself again; journeying deeper until it is unseen. He knows the lines are temporary and he is not going to let his opportunities for wonder disappear into the unseen. While contemplating his diverging and converging path, he doesn't hear the floorboards creek in the night.

"Grandpa, I have a question," a weary-eyed boy asks.

"Really? Do you now? Well then, I might just have an answer for you."

"Where do dreams go?"

"Ah! let me see if I can find it for you."

He looks around for a moment before pointing out towards the darkness.

"There," he tells him.

"Where?"

"There," he says again, still gazing towards the dark.

"Grandpa, where?? I can't see!"

"Ah, you're lucky. That means your dreams are right here," he says as he places a hand on the young child's heart.

"But where are the other dreams?"

"There…

if you start walking you'll find them all…

if you keep walking…

past the fears…

past the doubt…

past the despair….

past the anger…

past the irritation…

past the impatience…

past the thought…

past the hope…

past the belief…

past the knowing…

there…they're all there waiting."

"Waiting for what Grandpa?"

"Their dreamers."

Karmic

You're a leaf stuck to a web
Wildly dancing as the wind tries to pull you away
Are you holding on or trying to let go?
You see the spider and wonder from a distance
'What's keeping me in this play?'
She sees you and waits
For what?
For this
Whenever
Wherever
However
Whatever
For the one she knows will move you away from her
and closer towards you,
Watching you, she marvels,
"Your eighth leg is missing, not letting you fall
nor rise awake."

.tavisha

Find the king who holds love in his pocket

"I wonder, do you truly believe a roaring lion to be the king or a silent but anticipating one to be? Remember the king of time: one who moves like a gentle elephant, strong enough to create new streams but pure enough to softly walk and not disturb existence with unnecessary noise. One who is truly knowing usually moves in silence and surprises you because they don't need a parade to announce their presence. They're also not in a race against time, trying to get to a place before what they need is even there. A journeying king is not on an ego trip, he is not one who believes he is above the people under his guidance. He is one who is from the people and for the people, who is beyond the game of chess between black and white, who does not even exist in the spectrum in between, that's why you haven't found him in the greys yet either. Maybe you'll know when you die and metamorphosize, but you're not a rooted tree so do tire yourself from the swing of the victim and blame game. Sometimes it takes journeying to the bottom of our hearts to push past our boundaries which we use to hold ourselves in a ring; free from the coin flipping incessantly while you wait for a new face to emerge. Then on your one day, you'll realize how you're lucky the people the false king attacked still stand by you. And they only did because they see the shard of truth beneath the layers, the deceit. They'll let you play your game and sacrifice their pieces, but there will always be one part of them you can't kill and that's the part that sees the real you, the part that knows you. The parts of them thriving with love for you. Oh, my friend, you create a paradox when someone matches your movement with stillness, because you moved to move them, but your movement created the very stillness in them that then stills you."

.tavisha

Master of disguises

I was too quick to live my own life
Too eager to say my goodbyes
Held a heart broken and ready inside
For a love that future still has to hide

To all the friends I lost before it was their time
I'm sorry
To the ones I left unloved and blind
Sorry for this grieving heart's way to pull off any show
Without ever being held through the unknown

But do know I'm not sorry we weren't meant to be
I can't be the flow to your creek
Because separate we're not incomplete
Though I'm sorry you blame me
For breaking your love at its knees

The inversion you'd adore
Is not the immersion I long for
You know your love wasn't tall enough for mine to fly
in
But it's soft enough that your fallen heart will not
thin

I walked the cold just not too long I know
I laugh alone whether or not I belong
Because I left me out here all along
You know deserted lullabies mark my throne

And I know you still wish my soul never called me
home

Honestly, you've frustrated me
There is no justice in your anger for me
Because I made sure you knew so that you wouldn't
hold an empty care hopelessly
You don't have the right to claim I left you behind
Because all my life, I told you I'd happily spend my
entire existence alone
Than with a soul who doesn't harmonize with mine
And his, I told you
His, I knew before the existence of space and time

.tavisha

It's a common irrationality we may share

I don't want to be part of the mainstream

But the flow that just loses itself and goes free

Seeing all the bird families and trees

Oh, these trees the rushing stream see blurry

Sightseeing while I run dry

Not even realizing this is a die

Until I disappear with a heavenly sigh

And hope that at least some seeds will sprout because
of me

The little drop that tore herself apart from her sea

The one that believed she could dream

That one day she'd see their eyes welcome her stream

.tavisha

UNHEARD THROUGH THE NOISE

"Ha he! Ha he!" the crazy old man mutters, "Crazy crazy! CRAZYYYYYYY!! Eeeeeeee! Ouuu! AAAAAAAHHh..." His mumbles quickly turn into full blown screams, "OHHHHHHHHHHHH!!!!!!!!!!!!"

"WHAT is going on here!? Contain him! Strap him down! Crazy old man, stop with your noise today!" the Doctor says as he walks away.

Shouts of "HAAAAAAAAAA!" and "OUUUUUU" continue resonating through the halls anyway.

Night after night, his cries plague their ears. One night, the Doctor dares to go in with a shot and a threat, "If you do not stop screaming, I will inject you with a sedative and put you to bed."

"Ouuuuuuuuu," whispers the crazy old man.

The Doctor knows that the injection will do little in the long run. He drags himself back to his office where a pile of files and a bottle of pills are waiting. He ghosts past the files and reaches for his medicine. He has an array he can choose from: alprazolam, chlordiazepoxide, clonazepam, diazepam etc…

He falls into his chair and lets his head spill across the table. He was not always this way. When he had first started at this institution, he was eager to help people heal. But now he knows what these pills have become: temporary fixes. He knows because he now needs his own routine fix. He recalls the wailing patient, an ordinary man not unlike himself until this special moment he simply describes as 'his when' no matter the methods the doctors have used to pry. No one could comprehend his madness.

Out of confusion, he wonders aloud, "He was doing fine…he was finally coming around…now all he does is yell." Sometimes the best thing to do is ask, not tell.

The Doctor visits him again, "I don't understand, you used to sit in absolute silence. What is your new obsession with this noise? Tell me why?"

"YOOOOOouuuuuuuuuuuuuu nevEEEEEEEEEERRRRRRRR understood MY silence…"

"Well, now I cannot understand your noise."

"Listen!!!!!
AAAAAAAAAAAAAAAAAAAAAAAAAAAAAAAAAAAAAHHH
HHHHHHHHHHHH… AHHHHHHHHHH!!!"

"All I hear is noise??"

"That is not all you hear!!! And you say that I am the crazy old man," he stutters through his ghostly laugh.

Frustrated, the doctor leaves and the old man becomes quiet again.

The next night, he acts normal for this time's day and age. Although there are no screams coming from his room, the Doctor still feels the uneasiness of a mystery unresolved. He goes back to the patient's room and looks at him curiously.

"What do you need?" asks the crazy old man.

"I want to understand…"

"I said need not want, do not confuse the two."

"I need to understand."

"I cannot explain it for you."

With everything in life, each can have their own interpretations. If he wants to know the intentions, he'd have to understand the crazy old man.

"When you struggle to understand your very self, how on earth will you understand me? Are you willing to be me?" asks the man.

"Will you just try!?" pleads the Doctor.

"NOOOOOOooooooooooooooooooooooooooo~"

"Stop Screaming!!!"

"I will only if **you** cry."

"What?"

"TRYYYYYYYYYYYYYYYYYYYYYYYYYYYYᴙᴙᴙᴙ..."

"Fine," the doctor hesitates but lets out a scream anyway.

"NO! NO! NO! Do it right! Do it with purpose! Intent! If not, why bother try?!"

"AAAAAAAAAAAAAAAAAAAAAAAAAAAAAA AAAAAAAAAAAAAAAAAAAAAHHHHHHHHHHHHH HHHHHHHHHH..."

"This is the first time I have heard you sing a sound! Do it again! Again! Again! Again! Again! Again! Again!"

"Crazy old man!"

"AGAIN! Hold it for as long as you possibly can. Twice or thrice! Only then will you understand!"

"AHHHHHHHHHHHHHHHHHHHHHHHHHHHHH HHHHHHHHHHHHHHHHHHHHHHHHHHHHHHHHHHHHHHHHHHHᴴᴴ ᴴᴴᴴᴴᴴᴴᴴᴴᴴᴴᴴᴴᴴᴴᴴᴴᴴ.........AHHHHHHHHHHHHHHHHHH HHHHHHHHHHHHHHHHHHHHHHHHHHHHHHHHHHHHHHHHHHHHH HHHHHHHHHHHᴴᴴᴴᴴᴴᴴᴴᴴᴴᴴᴴᴴᴴᴴᴴᴴᴴᴴᴴᴴ...................…....AHHH HHHHHHHHHHHHHHHHHHHHHHHHHHHHHHHHHHHHHHHH HHHHHHHHHHHHHHHHHHHHHHHHHHHHHHᴴᴴᴴᴴᴴᴴᴴᴴᴴᴴᴴᴴᴴᴴᴴᴴᴴᴴ ᴴᴴᴴ......"

"What happened?"

"...wait...let me catch my brea-"

"Exactly!!! He He!!!!"

"Crazy...old man."

"You desperately needed to take a breath."

"We all need to breathe."

"Yes! Yes! Indeed! But it is only because you've taken that breath that you can now create another sound! OHHHHHH!!! And it's only because you poured yourself out and let your noise die that your new breath could come to life. How profound it is to live and die again and again!!"

Turbulent

Often, people are living rushed.
Theyaretryingtomoveasfastaspossiblewithout
realizing that in the pauses, magic occurs.
Try to get lost in the silence between your thoughts,
Stretch it out and feel the bubbles collapse
Like the rhythm in the rainfall.
Or should we let it all fall?
Would you drown?
Would you suffocate in the extremes?

.tavisha

Again

They must be mad coming for three,
Apathetic souls' demise all for blinding lies
Murdering over who has a claim to the end
Under the guise of almighty's pen
Waking up to moonshine rain
We can't explain what we know
Again and again and again
Guided by the moons' face warmed by the suns' grace
While every line, they take as an ace

They think they're sane letting their dreams die in
vain
Suffocating instead of being patient with their pain
With a striking clock and unforgiving luck
Surrendering their wings for they're addicted to their
sins
Willing to trade a dime for their life for kicks they'll
leave behind
Welcomed to the twisted game of life

Awakened by the fall
Walking between two clouds, unsure which direction
to take
No need to escape
Again again again
Lead by their soul's throbbing pulse locked in a chase

Don't you know that a sin is a win with a turn of the face?
Just remember the link that moves it all in place.

87

.tavisha

Showering

It's the hook between my skull and spine
That tells me all of this is not mine,
It's the twisting of my mind around,
As my weighting tongue falls to the ground.

Now all I see are
These swirling eyes,
The rooted lies,
Come find me when the oceans rise
Into the sky.

Your eyes were flowers wilting away
By the stretched hands and shadows which play
In the dreaded and deadened light of late
Oh, if only time had stayed.

Your eyes, they gleam,
Of angered envy,
The flowers they screamed,
As we stood trembling.

.tavisha

Only the one who placed the sword can move it

Let's soak the stars
In the rising mars
And pull the spin
Of embracing skin

I know both clocks lied
As the river dried
They created time
To sway all her tides

You let her walk alone
Without the stories grown
Repent your I don't know
Ignore your foolish glow

As you drink to fears
Which cracked your tears
Pouring praising cheers
From unfolded years

As you reach through song
You'll come too late
Her heart won't heed your call to wake
Her own star is near not far from fate

Death's sword hangs over her form
Ready to take her home alone
And because your hand is wrong

You can only reach through song

.tavisha

Built in, Nostalgic, Predisposed

I saw people building on the rooftop today
I wonder if they know others go there to build too
Not only moments of construction through
destruction
Not only moments of awe through wonder
Not only moments of joy through pain
Not only moments of silence through noise
Not only moments of love through absence

I know you don't need the explanation
But he needs to be heard
Are you willing to listen?
You won't when your heart is closed
So, he may trigger you to first unfold
From a bud to a bloom
Your true beauty shown
But you won't even be aware
Because all you'll be trying to do is
Catch further fragments that he bares.

.tavisha

FLY THROUGH THE SEA;

DIVE INTO THE SKY

"I am looking through the air to see you."

"Who?"

"The same way that I would look through the water to see you if we were immersed in the ocean again."

"Who? What?"

“Do you think the fish are aware that their perception of infinity is not true reality?”

“…”

“Imagine you were in the water; it would look as though the water never ends no?”

“Hm, yeah… I guess. What's the point of this anyways?”

“I don't know…but why don't the bottom dwellers swim? Why do they stay on the ocean floor? Do you think that the fish above look down at them and wonder too?”

“Wonder what?”

“Why they don't let go and let themselves float?”

“Why would the fish think that?”

“Because for them it is inherent, predisposed.”

“Hm…interesting.”

“Do you think that birds look at us and think the same thing?”

“Think what?”

“Think: Why do those bottom dwellers stay bound to the ground? Don’t they know how to let go and fly?”

“Do they care to think?”

“Well, what if they did? What if they decided to come down to the ground and walk with us; become our teachers?”

“But you can't –”

“And what if the humans they encounter try to explain the logic of why we can't fly and why it makes sense for us to walk? What if those birds listened to them and decided they would be safer walking too?”

"What are you saying? That birds wouldn't
fly? That they wouldn't keep me company
in the sky?"

"Well, I was walking the other day when I saw a bird
hopping about…"

"So?"

"So, imagine the bird existed in that world."

"One with no birds flying?"

"Yes. Imagine what would happen if that world
existed long enough!! No birds would know they can
fly anymore! But, they would still possess that innate
potential which could never leave them no matter how
deep they bury it inside."

"They don't know they can fly,
but they know they can fly?"

"Exactly!! We realize that the birds in our reality don't
really think of flying, they just inherently do. Imagine
if that bird I saw was brought into a world where no
one else can fly. How is it going to know it can? It
might have that silent nudging feeling inside that's
urging it to spread its wings, let go, soar. But every
time it tried to tell someone of how it wanted to swim
through the wind, no one else understood and no one
else believed it could. Does our first bird succumb to
believing it cannot fly after a few failed attempts; that
it's just like the others? I'm telling you that even if it
did, the bird would always have a knowing within that
it was meant to swim through the wind. I hope that
bird keeps trying and that when the world feels its
flight; I hope it inspires others to follow their own
silent knowing within."

"Trust me when I tell you that
when your bird flies, it won't know
what a wonder it is to the others."

"Why not?"

> "I've simply seen it happen every now and again. Those who fly don't realize the love they spark in other's eyes. I know you to be like this bird."

"Me? Why?"

> "Because the lens of who you are casts light into darkness and stays there long enough for others to see. So, I dearly want to know, if you were like me, how would you be?"

"If I was like you, I would move swiftly but softly through the skies. Travelling around the globe, immersing myself in it and surrendering to life wherever I go. I would remind the people that the sky too needs release as I let myself fall and paint their world once more. And upon each musical death there will be a rebirth; when I return to the skies carrying the essence of where my art lies. My form will change for I will never twice be the same. Some days I'll be dense but light so that I can join the sun to play hide and seek with children below. Some nights I'll be a veil for the moon's glow, keeping it company as it reveals the night's mystery. Oh…it seems I collapsed a potential future into this temporary timeline again. Oh well, as a cloud, I'd live in my own flow, not in resistance, but in harmony's instance, no matter my distance."

> "Though we are distant, you have always been witnessing my silent transformation and we shall stand by

you and protect you through your own
metamorphosis."

"You know, I promise to never leave you, but please
stay with me too, even when I've forgotten you and
me. I'll stay to watch you become the tears that fall
from the sky. I'll stay and watch you dry back into
who you are. Maybe you can make me understand
how to fly again because I have all these chains
latching onto my soul, holding me down. Ocean, you
fall just like me and with every tear I lost, I begged for
one less day, one less pain. But with every moment's
tear, I am blessed with one less chain. Still, time has
been stretched and I don't know how to fly anymore,
with or without these chains. There was a time when I
used to fight to belong to the air. I thought that my
resistance was my strength, but it was the birth of my
despair. I have fallen but I have yet to surrender
because I still wear the mask of fear, of anger, of
pretense. Pain is breaking through these layers and
when all my masks are shed, I will be free, but will I
know how to fly again? The truth is I have no idea
who I will be."

"Don't worry, we'll be together
from beginning to end and
through all our living deaths
cycling in and out our breath."

"You seem to know, but I also wonder if flying feels
better than hopping…if the other birds would come
down to find out if they saw how pure this little one
was. There must be new ways of moving we haven't
remembered yet. New ways for water to disappear and
reappear, for light to be cast and uncast."

"Friend, why
don't you ever tell me what you are?"

"Hahaha that's because I'm still trying to remember!"

"Well, how can I help?"

"You see, no one can. I think I've tried to ask for help before, for a mirror because I can't see my own décor. All they did was put me in a box, keeping me locked to their eyes forevermore, until they saw me still existing out of there. Confused, they opened their precious secret compartments and found me still there. And cloud! You should have seen their quiver when you entered the picture, creating a blind spot like the absence of air! Hide and seek was always fun until they grew tired of looking and forgot that I was still waiting there. But I can never leave, my source is a secret kept even to me. They were fools though, they all asked death where I go, so death naturally came in my way to watch how I'm still playing. Casting a winged beast that I would not deny, a mirroring cry entered our life, creating a void I could rest in, yes, another glass bubbled try. And an owl with falsified feathers, her skin envy green she tried to paint with baby pink, hid between in wait for the ripeness of a wake to claim my space. Until I shared the only thing I knew with her; that I walked a bridge others saw as a line as though it wasn't a divide. She thought this was how I reached myself so she placed a seed into her own mind to reflect into mine, disappearing the bridge, the shine, the light, the life that bore our time. This is when I came to you for I could not play hide and seek with my own eyes, with no difference between them open and closed, I forgot which breath I was taking or giving. Blind, I felt myself get wrapped into words of 'you're mine' like scaled patterns repeating through time. I wondered if we could sing a deserted lullaby before I died at the edge of the line

and only then did the catch of the tail twist the void
into infinity's familiar chime and I knew through all of
time we would always coincide!"

"This friend, don't you worry
she could just meet you before your
birth and blind your eye before the
search can even exist in time?"

"It's not a reason to hide but a fuel that ignites for the
greater the contrast, the deeper the night and the
brighter the bright."

"But, if you're all
alone now that I've gone and hid
behind, what do you do?"

"Oh, I'm playing peak-a-boo with my own eyes. Just
twist around or wait, I'm not sure if I'll be slower or
quicker but I'll be perfectly on time!"

The ocean's in the air

Tell your angels softly
All the things you'll leave behind, your story
Only crazy wishes fill this head of mine.
Slipping through the clouds of paradise,
When you and I were beyond this paradigm,
Finding ourselves lost inside time.

And they all said that we'd be lost before we're found,
Shifting roughly like a game that has us down,
Clouds igniting all our once upon a times,
Only when we live through our divine,
Holographic life, show me,
What's the point of this plight?
Don't sing me lullabies that try to hide my own eyes.

I dare not let my eyes linger there
Where you've escaped into the shadows
Embraced, there was a time
When I knew that you were mine
Then, our love was in the sky

Oh, whispered sweet times
Twirling outside my life,
And freedom in spaces
Only in my dreamscapes.

This is my deserted lullaby.
.tavisha

It wasn't me! It was an earthquake caused by a dinosaur!

My younger cousin at 4 taught me the true art of puzzles at 24

He carefully took his pieces and place them together like he was sowing a special mystery

He looked over the image he had to copy

And checked that our sections were still incomplete

Then showed us his with a demanding

Look at me! Look at me!!

The adults smile, not realizing the splendor of his masterpiece

Nothing flowed seamlessly

One piece from the first dinosaur and a piece from the third were squished together

Like a piece from the past forced into a hole that smothered its edges and polished it smooth before presenting itself to society

But the rest all fit perfectly

Though the image portrayed was an amalgam indeed

It was the truest mirror of reality I have ever seen

One person blended into another into creek into a bee

One piece of you lied in me

While three of me were in the tree

When I let my soul read his puzzle

I saw all the 'I am you's and 'you are me's

His puzzle incomplete had already set free

Amazed, I undid what I had thought finished

And placed the pieces where they wanted to belong

Not wondering what the image on the box told me

Not hesitating for almost too long

Oh! how I wish you had seen that masterpiece

Because the next day we came home to our puzzle
scattered on the floor

With shared delight for what new conceptions would be
born

.tavisha

"Come, let's play spin world!"

The first dance I learned was to spin free

With all my brothers dancing beside me

Eyes high and arms flinging 'round

Almost melodic, definitely wild

As though we were each immersed in our own magnetic
romance, definitely like a child

And the fall was always such a surprise

Filled with much panic and laughter

Our reluctance to pain easily washed away by our
eagerness to dance again and again and

Again

.tavisha

DEAR WHY

"Come inside right now!!" cries a worried aunt. She wears the heaviness of the day in her brow but cannot betray the twinkle of excitement in her eyes.

"Where is she now?" asks her previous guardian.

"Outside, laying on the ground."

He laughs as he tells her, "She is your twin after all."

"Yours too, now go get her before she falls ill."

***

"Sweetheart, what are you doing?"

"Looking at the sky!!"

"Come, let's go look from inside."

The child starts crying but does not understand why. He remembers how she once demanded to stay with the falling snow until there was just enough to create angels. He wonders if this time she shall command water angels to life. He looks to the sky then back at this daughter he's meant to guide. He smiles when he realizes that he cannot tell the difference between the raindrops falling from the sky and the teardrops falling from her eyes. Instead of bringing her inside, he lays down on the darkened roads beside her. Together, they stare at the stars above even though they are sheltered in grey.

After enough time has passed for her to trust that he won't take her inside, she asks, "Why does it rain?"

"You learned this in school. Remember the water cycle?"

"I know, but that's how it rains. So, WHY does it rain?"

"I don't know, do yo—", his response cut off by a flashing light followed close by a thunderous clap. Scared and frazzled, she runs to the woman waiting inside.

***

After putting her to bed, her two shields find themselves staring outside again. He sees how much she loves the storm. He sees how whenever the lightning strikes, her eyes become warm.

"Why does it rain?" he asks.

She smiles as she replies, "I think the clouds get heavy and feel the need to release. I feel the same way sometimes. I think we all do. It's beautiful that the clouds cry. Too much and our world would drown, too little and we would not survive long. And then the light can shine again; if only as rainbows through the tears."

"She felt scared because of lightning's flash and thunder's roar," he says as he remembers the flicker of fear which compelled the little girl to run and hide.

"I used to get scared too. Do you know that they are not separate, but one and the same? Do you feel it shake your chest like an earthquake shakes the ground?"

"The way angered pain flashes through people sometimes," he says knowingly.

"But we don't need to fight our anger and sadness. The lightning lights up the dark so that we can see for a moment. Perhaps the thunder wakes us up to make sure we are seeing. That is what anger can do, it can wake up fragmented parts of you. We just need to be careful where our own lightning strikes."

"She asked me, 'Why does it rain?' outside."

"We were upstairs with the baby. He started crying and she closely followed suite."

"Why do you think she was crying?"

"Because she saw him crying. Then, it started raining and I asked myself aloud, *'Now, is the sky crying because it saw you crying?* Next thing I know; she's on the ground outside trying to understand why."

Hours pass by as they peer at the clouds blending into the sea.

"We can know how, when, where, what, but why...? Can we ever know why?"

"I don't know. Sometimes we think we know. With answers of survival being the typical, but then, there are those who ask, why survive? And those who seek to know what always survives, only then to wonder in a different way, why is it still here? Why survive? Why? Still, you can always go deeper in the ocean of who you are. And there, you'll find that you can always rise higher into the skies of your 'whys'. It's our infinity travelling through our eternity which either exists completely or unnecessarily in every moment, just as humans do I guess. Knowing why stopped bothering me when hope found me; hope that one day I will live with an awe that doesn't pause to wonder."

"I mentioned that she still has a flicker of fear in her, but do you know that she's still refusing to see."

"Really? Why and how would she do that?"

"Well, I may have shown her how to face the mirrors, but she still avoids looking into her eyes. Sometimes I wonder if she creates these thorns so that fear stays her friend."

"Dear friend, it is not fear she is seeking but the trust before believing. I will show her slowly."

"What if she is not ready?" he asks with a smile.

"You! You are the one who is not ready," she replies.

"Well, you're not one to judge! How many deaths have you refused her?" he teases with a laugh.

She sighs as she replies, "You see, we all forget who we truly are within that shell of a child, but together we'll remember."

"To think, if it wasn't for her, the lion and hippopotamus would have never been friends."

I'm ready to let me know my own my soul
Knowing I could throw it off the edge of the universe and
it would still remain whole

I remember how you said the moon could bend and break
again
And again, I looked at the sky and saw your eyes
But you're not here, I don't know if you're even there

Your back turned to mine as our cycle began
Pouring our tries to unite in the end, was it all pretend?
Because I'm still here, but you don't know that I'm here

Oh, come on now my love, I'll lighten our luck
Remember the times we sat in the cave
Talking for days by the ocean that kept us at bay
Telling stories about the birds we saw flying away

.tavisha

Confounded

I've gotten lost in the rainbows emerging from my lashes
Quietly wandering, seeking home in everyone's eye
Leaving a trace of my soul in every moment behind
Hoping it'll also lead him home so I can finally be found
Oh, but this mirror of mine has yet to be formed

So in our meanwhile,
The ocean's infinite depth is trying to show me my own
The fire's spiraling blaze is trying to shock me awake
The air's swirling void is trying to meet my pain
And the earth's quaking cross is trying to make me feel
whole

But I can't forget the ripple I've been swirling around
Is it me? Is it you? Is it merely a sound?
Is it free like the tree that was cut from the ground?
Or is it rooted like a soul that has always been bound?
What's the eye of the I that has yet to be found?
Can I know with a head that has yet to be crowned?

Though my soul is desperate to be known,
The ocean's infinite depth couldn't show me my own,
The fire's spiraling blaze couldn't shock me awake,
The air's swirling void couldn't meet my pain
And the earth's quaking cross couldn't make me feel
whole

My mirror, oh yes, it'll take my own soul
For me to come home, finally known
.tavisha

Like a fool

You won't fool a fool who's been set free
You won't hand a fruit from the tree
Like an ornament you carried instead
Of mending the seeds in your head

Long the mirror held the stare
Of a heart turned cold's glare
A life born unprepared
From a soul stripped bare

They took your song and turned it wrong
They struck our luck, turned fire into mud
Caused the blankets to fall between my lives
One for the world, one for my mind
The stars ablaze deep in the night
But then come day, they fall from sight

Then, our mind and bodies don't get along
As I walk around like a human paradox
My mind tells me to fight while my body stays calm like
a night
Because my anger abandons me in moments the world
says matter
And finds me in benign times when my tongue tenses up
and my mind says shut up

But you'll pick me up like stolen daffodils

And you'll write my life with a pen that lost its skill
Turn me around on a wheel till I fall in
Then set me free, crying
I'm not moving, I'm flying
As my body settles into dust
What a fool I am for bearing a fool's trust.

My minds don't get along
Caught in a tug of war using my bones as rope
One likes to ride the slippery slope
The other likes to hope

Like a fool, my heart sings along to the eye that holds
hope
Like a fool, my soul seeks for a love still unknown.

.tavisha

WINDOW

The man is almost at the end of his arduous journey where he finds himself haunted by doubt as questions fly through his mind, *"Did I choose the right path? What if this really is an unlived life's crisis like my mother insisted? Was I crazy to leave everything and come here? What am I even searching for?"*

It has been eight hours since his eyes have seen the common ground. Though he lapses in and out of the illusion that the fog has joined him in the sky, his feet are now completely surrounded by clouds. But he isn't lost in it, for his skin matches the softness of earth and not the translucence of fog. It has been a long journey indeed and with every pressing moment, he can feel the weight of his life curve his spine. He wonders why he left the stability of his old life behind. Now, he lives always seeking and never staying for he knows there is always something new to find.

He finally makes it to the opening of the cave, when someone yells, "STAY RIGHT THERE!! Don't move!" The man had been warned of the Master who calls this cave home. He's generally known for not belonging to any conventions of the norm. The man freezes, blocking the mouth of the cave, as he proceeds to ask, "Do y-"

"Be quiet. Don't speak. Don't move." the Master commands, as he lays down and closes his eyes. Some would be exasperated to be welcomed with such a command, but the young man is ecstatic. He's eager that his training is beginning right away.

Standing there, silently waiting, he sees the sun rising in the sky and feels lucky for he had started his hike early enough in the day. He waits for hours as the sun makes its own journey higher. He invites the warmth it brings, but it soon starts burning his skin. He ignores the singeing pain for as long as he can but escapes to the shadows in the cave within the fifth hour. Quietly, he walks to the Master to observe his technique, but his jaw quickly loosens, for the Master is asleep. He gives him a rough shake as he mutters through a clenched jaw, "For the last few hours, you've made me stand in the scorching sun just so you can sleep!?"

The Master lets out a long yawn stretched by the echoes within the walls. "Did you see the light dance?" he asks with a hopeful grin.

The man grinds his teeth to release some of his inner pressure then answers, "I saw the sunshine create shadows which had been hidden in the dark."

"No," the Master leans in. He leans in close enough to the man to make him feel uncomfortable, "Did you see the light dancing?" The man looks at the Master and worries himself with thoughts that the villagers were right. He can feel his tension rise to the back of his neck and wonders if he should leave right now to save the rest of his day and perhaps salvage his life.

He decides to grant the Master one more chance. "No, I didn't see the light dancing, or maybe I did, but I don't understand what you're asking. The light dancing with what? On wha-" The young man stares in bewilderment as the Master rolls around, shaking the air with his deep bellied laughs. This time, he cannot control the pressure which swiftly passes through him and seethes through his words, "why. are. YOU. LAUGHING!?" he silently roars.

When the Master can finally breathe again, he explains, "The light dances with itself! Oh, how I wish you had seen. Oh, how I hope you will see."

The living laughter trying to change his anger's course tenses him to the sharpened point of rigidity. "If you had told me what to look for, maybe I would have seen it. Isn't a Master supposed to guide others?"

"Who told you that? Even if a master tells you what to look for, you may still not see it. If I tell you what you're looking for, you will definitely not find it."

"Then you're not a good Master," he says quite abruptly.

"Perhaps," the Master says thoughtfully, "or perhaps, you're not a willing student."

The man, utterly confused, mutters, "I watched the sun rising while I was waiting for you. You! You, who made me stand there so you could sleep some more!"

"Perhaps I was living through the illusions of the eye and believed the darkness you cast came from the sky. Anyways, you're not yet the you that will find anything," he evenly states. The Master can sense that the young man is irate, but that his mind still doubts if this is part of a training. To appease his fire, the Master beckons he ask the question he had tried to ask earlier.

"Do you have an ego?" he asks, curious as to how this Master will answer in comparison to all those he had learned from prior.

"I do not have anything, but this form, I must temporarily hold," the Master responds.

A usual answer, from an unusual Master, but said with such softness that he can already feel the tension being released within himself; as though he is entering a mindful trance.

"Please, tell me how to get rid of the ego."

"You may have read many books on the subject, you may have attended many sessions on the matter, you may have met many masters of the ego, you may have met many egos of the masters, but do you know what '*yours*' means?"

"I know it's there, I just don't know how to get rid of it. That's why I came to you, everyone who speaks with you leaves with a light in their eyes. You must know something."

"Realize knowing that 'something' exists and knowing it are not the same. Many people today are arguing over the question, 'What?' and not allowing themselves to pay attention to 'How?' and 'Why?'. Those answers, you already have yet you still want a journey."

"And what of the questions, 'Where?' and 'When?'"

"Here and now, of course!"

"Please, you must help me see the answers," he begs. He knows he is different from the phantoms he embodied before. When he discovered the shards in himself, he almost got lost in unfathomable distress. But now, he keeps discovering new pieces of himself and thus cannot find himself whole. "Please, I cannot keep living like this. I feel as though sleep's curtain warms me with its embrace but stops me from seeing the light it keeps at bay. I'm scared to jump into this unknown because I do not know where I will land, but I know that I cannot remain in my emptiness. Please help me, I feel as though someone has put a blindfold on my soul."

"You've been looking through a window that has been darkened and it has distorted your view of reality."

"How do I clean the window?"

"No. No. No." The Master swats at the man's hands as though he is but a child who has reached for forbidden fruit, "Do you know what darkness is?"

"It is when there is no light! I have heard this before! 'Darkness is the absence of light'."

"Does darkness only exist when there is no light?"

"No–"

"Does light exist because of the darkness?"

"No…wait…yes…Wait, I know this–"

"Temporary and fleeting, aren't they?"

"What?"

"Your thoughts."

"Do you know the light only because you know the dark?"

"I'm confused. Please, slow down, you're asking too fast."

"Does one exist without the other?" the Master asks, making a point to stretch out each sound until it's just barely comprehensible.

"Yes," the man replies in a controlled tone as to not reveal his annoyance, but he can't stop himself from adding, "There's no need to be childish. If you speak too fast, I can't understand you, but if you speak too slow, I won't understand you."

"Is it only by understanding the words I speak that you understand me?" the Master asks, adding an audible, "You've forgotten your desire to be childlike," quickly moving on before the man can reply, "Darkness and light. Is the idea of one understood without the other?"

"I don't know."

"It is understood by those who don't seek to look to see, but who simply look and therefore, see. You are right in saying that the absence of light creates darkness, but you don't understand what you speak. There is a source of light within you, but there is no source of darkness. Or is there?"

"Perhaps I can't see through the window because it is dark out there, not because the window itself is dark or because it is dark in here?" the man asks, fearing that the Master is merely toying with his mind and will let him leave with more confusion than he entered with. His doubt is already transforming into dread and he worries it will soon become regret.

The Master can sense what is clouding the man's mind and tells him, "Infinite paths can be taken to understand why, but to understand begins with awareness. Now, you know how."

"Just awareness? Isn't that too easy?"

"As others have already told you, bring your awareness to the observer. The observed observer. The aware awareness."

"You are merely mirroring words now."

"See! The answer you seek is already within. Even now as you say the words aloud, you have not recognized the freedom in embracing "I don't know" rather than a false "I know" or a confused "I should know". Pay attention to what you think is darkness…and you'll see shadows forming…and you'll know the eternal light shining."

"Then, I'll see through the window: true reality?"

"No. And do not forget that you are not only an observer but also an active participant."

"A participant in what?"

"In the creation you call your life of course," the Master says as if this knowledge is obvious.

"So you're saying that I have to clean the window endlessly? That can't be right, you're just making this up," he exclaims while desperately trying to let go of his fear that the Master may confirm this mental slavery. The Master walks softly to the cave's eye and whispers gently to the man inside, "Do what you will, until you finally realize that the window you've been looking through is a mirror which longs to be still."

The man, having had enough, throws himself to the ground, beating in its flat existence. The Master comes around, picks him up effortlessly and tosses him out. "When you hurt your mother, you reveal the hurt within yourself. Leave."

"No, no..no," he whispers, "Please, see, this is why I need your help"

"No."

"Please, I have nothing."

The Master looks at the trembling man before him and decides to give him another chance. After all, life continually grants us new chances, even if through a full bellied Master like him.

"Fine, leave and journey to the bottom of this mountain. Then turn and travel back up. Do this 9 times. Do it until you can barely move forward, until you cannot move, then do it again. If you come back and show me that you can make the journey again, I will send you back."

The young man's eyelids peel back but his nod holds the determination of someone who will receive what he came for.

***

On the first journey, he rushes with a bounce in his step, as if someone has electrocuted newfound life into him.

On the second journey, he walks a little slower, taking in the air around him.

On the third journey, he takes wistful pauses without the need for causes.

On the fourth, he grows thirsty for something to hold dear.

On the fifth, he notices the sun's heat robbing him of his water and curses it.

On the sixth, he takes a different path, follows an animal, and finds a creek of water.

On the seventh, he goes back to his original route. He notices the army of clouds coming his way and knows they will obscure the light of the sky. They will also cleanse the mountain of his footprints, leaving him without his past as a guide.

On the eighth, he hears a choir of snakes and has to change his way again.

On the ninth, he stops at the mountain's feet. He looks up at the mountain he had almost left abruptly and turns as he readies himself for the climb again. It will be different this time, he thinks. The moon will soon peak out from the veil of light and reveal secrets of the night. He freezes for a moment, feeling the paralyzing unknown, but shakes it off and puts one foot forward.

As he looks up, he sees the cave's opening. It resembles an eye, if an eye could oversee all. He compares his position to the mountain's eye and realizes that he is standing near the mountain's heart. He leans across a tree nearby; staying there so long that it engraves its wisdom on his skin. The whispers of a breeze let the tree's leaves speak to the others. It is time for him to start feeling in his deadened spine, they say.

He doesn't know how he will carry himself forward when he can't carry himself straight without the help of this tree. He wishes that the wind would help him, not knowing that it already had. He turns and looks at the flickering lights of the village. He sighs for he knows he cannot go back down there. He will not go back down into that madness, that abyss.

He commences an inner dialogue similar to one parents adopt when encouraging a child who is just learning to walk. His thoughts carry him back to the creek where he knows the throat of the mountain would be singing. His thoughts have simmered down in the last hour, his resilience wearing thin for he is fighting the world with as much success as a baby fighting sleep in their mother's loving arms. Still, without knowing how, something carries him forward.

Upon his ninth return to the cave, he tries to find the Master, but against all will, his body collapses to the ground. He tries to move his arms, his knees, his head, but every effort is met with struggle. This battle goes on until he lays there in paralysis. He feels his presence spread from his body to the cave's edges. He is wary of what might happen if it finds its way to the cave's opening. *"Will I dissipate and exist no more?"* he wonders. Tears pierce his eyes, but the stings penetrate his whole body. Then, everything stops. He feels himself surrender and begin his death.

When the illusions cease to be, he opens his eyes and sees the Master hovering over him.

"Do you remember what you asked when you first arrived?" he asks.

"About?"

"Yes. Do you understand now?"

He rubs his eyes as he tries to find the stability of the ground vibrating with life below him. He looks closer and can see the air vibrating too. Suddenly, he feels a pain in his shoulders. The Master had quickly grabbed him with his heavy hands.

"Lose your mind!" he commands, "Do you need another shove down the mountain? You're still seeking a key when there is never any lock!"

Before he can reply, the Master throws a sharp rock bound by angular faces while revealing, "No one is a teacher or your enemy, understand we are all friends who continue meeting in infinite ways. Appreciate the mirror of this weighted rock and you will transcend. The understanding will not come from you, so your journey here is simply to receive it." The Master then gently shoves him to ready him for a new climb. As he softly falls to the ground, he can see the blur of trees rushing by. He feels a new surrender, one without resistance, for once you've been swallowed by momentum, what else is there to do but give in?

**Don't worry about your mistakes and missteps in this
dance; they were coincidental: on purpose both from
the beginning and from the end**

If you believe in god as all that is,
Then you're all the messiahs awaiting yourselves
Remember the flow of divinity doesn't exist for
exclusivity's sake

And if you don't,
Then a different path, do take.
They encourage science as a way or
Merrily just play;
They all lead to the same anyway.

And one day,
You'll meet those you saw blinded by faith,
And those you envied for envy's sake,
But, I do hope, on your journey to your wake,
You don't forsaken love even when you think it's too
late.

.tavisha

It all comes back to you

You kiss her hand to see if she will look at you
But her eyes too soon had found her mirroring clue
Golden fire to waving blue, they dance between the
two
Then he's gone as quick as found but then
She knew he knew...he always knew

You threw your expectations like seeds that could
land
And grow into a secret garden you could open with
only your hand
But this love burns fiercer and won't give a grown
shadow for you to hide in
Now, who has been walking and lying and dying?

Don't cut the snakes sistering like a ribbon
Don't charge the hounds for one is hell and one is
heaven
When you don't know your life's in shadows truly
golden
You will lust instead of love, you won't glow
Because in love, you don't think, you know.

.tavisha

Through lavender fields

Through lavender fields
Walk sages with dreams
Their souls flying high
On a winter breeze

They told you goodbye
Said your life's not a lie
The ladder was nigh
And you climbed it alive

Backwards and blind
Undead through your love
You went more above
Than the wings of a dove

And the journey unseen
By knights who gleam mean
Drawing arms for a fight
Seeking the jewel of their night

From the ocean between
Churning stories through dreams
Desires burning a new fire

For no one could be her sire

But from the other side of her shore
A mystic sings her home
Alone he knew her unknown
His moonlight's grace unsown

.tavisha

FORGOTTEN FRAGRANCE

"The easiest things we feel are the hardest to explain," repeats the gardener.

"What things are easy to feel?"

"Oh, you know… hunger, happiness, sadness, anger, pain, …love…"

The gardener sneaks one look at the warrior and knows that her words are not lost on her. Siaham stands there with a special smile on her face as though her presence is far away yet still here pulsing in the air. She knows that she is almost ready to leave. She can only hope that she will not hide from her destiny.

"Have you ever been happy?" she asks her guide.

"Yes."

Siaham glances towards the pastures. The grass has grown long enough that you can see its waves when the wind rushes by. It is a sight that has always soothed the waves within Siaham, but today the wind moves gently, softly sending shivers down her spine.

"Are you happy right now?" the gardener asks as she works her way into the ground.

"I am," she replies while maintaining her gaze towards the sky.

"How do you know?"

"Well…I don't know. I look at the sky and immediately I smile. A reflexive smile is a sign that I am happy the same way that the smoke is a sign of fire isn't it?"

"So, you think you know because you're smiling?"

There is a long pause between the two. She continues working the ground while Siaham tries to battle her doubt. She knows what is true. She knows when she is happy, but how to explain this is still an unknown mystery to her.

She admits defeat as she delicately reveals, "No, I've smiled through my tears before. I've even smiled when facing fear."

"Then, how do you know?"

Siaham continues peering into infinity. "*The sky is a blend of pastels because the Sun is saying good night. Soon, the darkness will set in, but we will still see infinity. Right now, the hues look like they go on forever. You can't see the darkness that exists after; it looks like the light is all there is,"* she thinks.

"I look at the sky and see infinity. I'm happy because I wonder; because I listen to the mystery. Yet, I don't know how I know and I don't know how to explain it to you."

"But you know nonetheless."

"Yes. Do you know that I am happy right now?" asks the girl.

"I do," replies the gardener.

"How?"

Siaham gasps. She doesn't know how but she can feel her teacher in her. She knows what she's feeling, she breathes in her thoughts of hope that the deer will come home again and maintain the harmony that once bound all creatures here. This feeling lasts only a moment, but it is enough. Siaham falls as she gasps for air, having forgotten to breathe in the moment of wonder. She can still feel her blood dancing inside, which the wind seems to also know for it suddenly becomes powerful enough to cool her skin and calm her fire.

Siaham controls her breath as the woman tenderly caressing the ground reveals, "I can feel it because it resonates through you and ends with sparks in your eyes."

"Is this how you know even when I can't explain it?" she enquires.

"Some choose to explain because they don't express. Their words are empty; they lack the soul's sincerity. I can feel your happiness because there is a stillness within me which allows me to be present with you right now; there is no need for you to explain."

"Then why ask me the question?"

"I wanted to know how you think. And I wanted to know if you were ready or if you would pass out again."

"Again?"

"Yes, again. I cannot tell you how many times we have been through this, but each time you wake up from that deep sleep, you've forgotten."

"Forgotten what?"

"You know what," she says with sternness, but Siaham didn't know. Although she feels there is treasure within her, she has forgotten how to remember and this absence of a presence she once knew has been haunting her.

"I have learned that although meaning can be lost in translation, most times it is lost in interpretation. I wish you hadn't asked me if I think I know because I do not think when I know. This sense of knowing is hard to explain. I know when I am happy, I know when I am sad, I know when I am hurt, I know when I am… I don't have doubts floating around in my mind when I know but sometimes the very question creates hesitation in me."

"Ah, yes. But we don't need to have that conversation again. You remembered! And when you remember, there is no need to relearn. You already know. Why don't you ask me a question?"

Siaham's body sighs as she softly says, "There will be times when we don't receive answers to the questions we ask."

She remembers the soul her dreams keep finding, "There will also be times when we receive answers to questions we have yet to ask." The warrior observes the gardener as she tends to the fruit. She knows that she will soon have to leave; set off on her journey. She saw it in her guardian's mind, even though she had tried to block her off from it. She lays down with the earth and feels herself sink in. She wishes she could stay here forever because the world with this gardener feels like home. But she can't keep hiding. As Lily had said when Siaham first arrived,

"No one will know where to find you and no one will be looking for you because no one even knows you're gone yet." But upon the look of relief on Siaham's face, Lily went on to say, *"But, you will not stay here forever. Don't worry, you can stay as long as you need, but when you're ready, you will know you need to leave."* That conversation often seeped into Siaham's dreams, but it appeared more so lately since the time to leave has come near.

Siaham lets out a sigh. She's ready to bear it all because she knows getting out of her own way is the way to survive. No matter how many times she needs to learn the lesson, it always ends the same; with another part she foolishly thought was her destroyed for her to get closer to the whole.

"Do you love these flowers?" she asks as she stares in delight at the jade vines hanging on the branches nearby. They remind her of her ocean; an ocean that she has been waiting for. That tree is where Lily had found her while she took refuge from the storm that was her life years go. She doesn't remember how that desert turned from a soft orange wasteland to the wonderful forest she finds herself in now. All she remembers is seeing one flower emerge, then another one, then another and another until it seemed she was standing in a vast sea of these forgotten flowers. Almost swiftly, she was no longer lost in a desert, but lost in a magnificent but just as vast paradise.

"Yes," the gardener laughs, "I think you'll soon be leaving me."

She continues to stare off into infinity knowing full well that it can be found anywhere, in any space, any time, and anyone's eyes. She continues looking at the jade vines, wishing she could see those eyes once more.

"Aren't you going to ask me why I like flowers?" Lily asks as she moves towards her tree.

"No."

"Why not?"

"Why does it matter? Some things are not for me to understand. Whether you like mangos or not has nothing to do with me."

"You're sad about leaving me, but you have always known your destiny," she reveals, softly adding, "I will always be with you whether you remember it or not."

"Do you love mangos?" Lily asks her.

"Let's pretend I've never seen one. What does it look like?" Siaham asks with a coy smile, "What does it feel like? What does it smell like? What does it taste like?"

The gardener stares at her in wonder. Her eyes do hold infinity. All she has to do is find her eternity.

"Can't explain it, can you?"

"I can try, but it wouldn't do," Lily shares.

"Yes, you can try. You can describe it in infinite ways. You can explain its structure, its history, its colour, its texture…but if you start explaining, we will be here forever. Yet still, you know it. You know."

"Yes…and no matter how well I explain it, the only way you will understand is by smelling, seeing, feeling, and tasting it yourself; by experiencing it as only you will. But I'll tell you what is really bothering you love. The only way you can know his soul is by knowing your own."

"I know…and once it's known, it cannot be unknown right? Not again?" she replies as she gathers the courage to say goodbye, "I know that what I have been searching for is a fruit I tasted long ago but can't seem to remember. Your flowers saved me and now I understand them. There are moments in life when it seems as though our external world is crumbling. These moments are not limited nor restricted by time. These moments are the powerful opportunities for inner flourishing. We're like these flowers; constantly sprouting beyond the seed and growing; taking nourishment from our roots and from above. We do blossom and we do crumble within ourselves to return to the earth. We are forever growing, blossoming, and returning. A constant rhythm of inhalation and exhalation. It really is beautiful."

"Earlier, I thought. Now, I know that you are ready to go." She hands her a newly bloomed white aster as a reminder while wiping a falling tear from her face. "The last morsel of truth you need before you leave are these flowers. They are like your thoughts. They do not float in and out. They do not emerge. Your soul moves to witness them."

"Will I remember any of this?"

"Before you go, I'll let you remember this: As much as you want to ride with the wind, remember that you can always pause on the wind and trust where it leads you. The rest you will remember as you unfold."

"Unfold?"

"You may be a bud that has yet to unfold, but remember, you cannot force a flower to bloom before its time. Once your spine is aligned, the harmony of nature within you will abide and unravel. And your blossoming will be divine."

As she speaks, the petals of the flowers start drifting off into a birthing wind which also carries Siaham's soul. No one can selfishly keep the truth from being alive, so Lily knowingly goes back to tending her garden, seeding new hope that these flowers will unfold again.

It also came to pass

Jealousy is part of our shell, tattooed in your hell,
Wishing the other existed only for you,
Wishing the other exists still for you,
But I can't take the world's shining star,
Even if I knew from the first moment your voice called my soul,
With no face, no form, nothing but your melody calling me
home,
Though you tricked me with your shadowed eyes,
I saw that flicker of gold light,
My world's devil; but an angel in disguise,
Fine, if you only want to meet in the skies,
I'm cutting our ties,
But I'll never let go of my night,
Because that is what welcomed my star home
And shed the cloudy waves from my ocean's eyes.

.tavisha

Wrangled by that page's spell

If a book was withheld from you

Until a page could be removed

One that would catalyze love

Or make a beginning undone

I would worry but

Do not fret over a hole in a story

For that page will become a bird

A bird that cannot fly

For her wings are made of wooden feathers

So, set yourself on fire

And be born from ashes of unmoving times

For that's the key to opening your treasure mind

A page that was ripped and well-kept inside

One glimpse of free chimes, one you have yet to find.

.tavisha

Dashing

I hope you find one who swarms around you

And makes you feel warm

Like a song that's finally found its home

I wonder, were you ever mine to hold?

Carefully I lock my soul

Slowly hoping you'll call once more

Knowing the clouds will not pour

Won't bare my moon anymore

I skip through thoughts I used to pause on for you

And drink to the spells my mind and heart spewed

Cheers darling, I celebrate you too

Just as a withering bloom

.tavisha

I told you I'd turn this into a poem, knowing me

I was erasing my candid moments with a fearful
What if someone sees?
Under the illusion of being watched
I act guarded
I do my least
Unpulled smiles became rarer

But I feel a release
Only because I have you to lean on
Thank you loves
It doesn't matter if I understand
Through you, I learned that commas make a difference
Even though I forget to pause when I'm with you

You still love that my eagerness contradicts my calmness
To the point that you lose letters in the end
Though you told me our contradiction is merely an interaction
Like dreams of fire drinking in water and growing

We were stubborn one moment and vulnerably willing the
next
We listened to each other's extravagance and believed in
each other more than ourselves
It was easy to see the radiance of your soul always shining
through

Though it was easier for me to tell you the universe wouldn't
be the same with your absence
The truth is, I won't be

You held my closed hand and now I'm telling you
Thank you love
For your existence reassures me

.tavisha

Reflecting faith

Trust is a question we ask of ourselves
To find the answer within we knew all along.
You meet it on the way to believing,
But by then it won't matter,
You'll jump in and fly when they fall.

.tavisha

here ; now

FALL

Looking back, it seems that everyone already knew, everyone except for me.

***

The plane is almost there. The people around me express an eclectic mix of emotions as our guide announces that the doors are soon going to open. Following this announcement, one member of our group runs to the far end of the plane. As I make my way towards the cowering man, I realize that his anxiety is trapping him for he is shaking within his skin and his spirit is dripping with dread.

"Why are you scared?" I ask him.

"I thought I was ready to experience this, but I was wrong, I don't want to jump."

"You don't need to be scared. If you don't want to jump, no one else can force you here."

The man stops trembling for a while as I think to myself that he will be back soon enough. Once you have started the journey, you will always come back to it. It will continue to nudge you forward like a thorn within your being.

The doors open, revealing an ocean whose soul dances to the moon but mirrors the sun's rays. The vastness of the world before us brings tears to my eyes. I look to my side to find another man crying though his tears tell stories of unwillingness.

I ask him, "Are you alright?"

He looks straight ahead and tells me, "I can't do this."

Before joining the first man, I tell him gently, "If that is so, then you are not wrong."

I look around and see someone looking down.

I go to her and ask, "Are you going to jump?"

"I want to feel the fall, but what if…I don't know…"

"Do you trust the unknown?" I ask her.

"Honestly, I do not. Yet, I still want to jump."

"If you cannot trust the unknown, then find something you can. Do you trust the inventions of man?"

"Yes, I do trust the parachute."

"Do you trust in your ability?"

"Yes, I know I will be able to deploy it."
But as she says this, I feel her grow suspicious of me. Although we had exchanged friendly conversation before takeoff, fear easily takes over as her soldier and projects thoughts to protect her.

"She probably wants me to jump first to see if I survive....or she wants me to not survive, maybe she knows something I don't, after all who am I to know who to trust... no I won't be jumping today, I'll come back when this woman isn't here," she thinks before leaving me alone again.

I look at all the people behind me and see how they are all past versions of me. This hesitation to live has been guarding me for far too long.

The first person I spoke to felt fear before the doors were ever open. He made himself comfortable as far away as possible. He ran away from the idea of falling the instant it began calling. The second person I spoke to felt fear because he had seen outside the door. Sometimes, the less one knows, the easier it is to let go, but that requires a trust in the unknown. The third person I spoke to felt fear of an end below. She was aware of the possibility of not surviving. In these people, I see fear of a future when it is merely a possibility. They do not realize that anticipation is beautifully dangerous; it is not trying to imprison them but merely seduce them forward.

I look out to the beckoning blue. My prolonging hesitation will be the death of me, but I have already fallen out of sync with what has been told. I close my eyes and let myself go, knowing now that the moment a free fall turns into flight has been seeking me all my life. I must release my hold of it all to feel the flight in my fall.

Let the veils fall.

Soon fear will no longer be here nor there
Not as a motivator nor as a punisher
In that moment, you will learn
For to motivate yourself to live
Leads to a life lived asleep
But to let yourself be inspired by existence
Leads to a life that is filled with essence.

There are many who exist,
Desperately thirsty for their dreams,
But should the oasis present itself,
Before the person in question,
Would *it* drink *it* in?
Because there are many who exist,
Who are more afraid of living
than they are of dying.

But do remember,
Our hearts were fused by whispers
Promising to fragment into crystalline
Droplets before melting into you and me

.tavisha

Standing behind

Can you build a home without a house?
One that's free and wild like a child
Build it slow, it'll make for such a show
When you're late, silence frames what they don't know

Can you leave the sincere uninvolved?
They don't know the emptiness of love
How it's smaller than a ray from up above
Yet brighter than the burning fire's sun

You glow without the moonlight shine
Sparkling honey like you're divine
You're one of few, at least that's true
Until they think they'll rescue you

This one's for you my baby blue
Embedded in a fragment's clue
Promise you'll let me fall in too
Shed your mask, tell me you're you

.tavisha

REFLECTIONS

"How many stories can you see?" asks one teacher to another.

"In what?"

"It doesn't really matter what. Let us look at this glass. What do you see?"

"A glass containing water."

"Now, what can you see?" asks the teacher without changing a thing.

"I still see a glass filled with water."

"Yes, I know, but what else **can** you see? Any story?"

"I don't quite follow. What can you see?"

"The glass is filled with water, which is what we need to stay alive. However, some care more about the glass than the substance contained within. I understand how powerful the mind is for I have seen many before me believe the water tastes better because of the vessel it's in."

"What if I push this off the table and the glass breaks. What do you see then?"

"I understand that some may see a life that could have been. I see that some may blame the hand for pushing the glass and others may blame gravity, but I recognize the dichotomy. There is a dance between the laws of nature and the creatures within it."

"What if someone walks on the glass? What do you see then?"

"I see how people are quick to judge yet slow to understand. The person who pushed the glass realizes their role in the glass shattering due to our relationship with time. Should someone walk by and carry glass off with their feet, who knows what can happen and why? It may seem far away, but the hand that pushed the glass will still be part of the play."

"What if someone tries to clean the glass and cuts their hand? What do you see then?"

"I see an artist's mark on those who live on. Some may rush to the glass and try to mend it back to life. They will learn that the glass cannot contain the water again; it was merely a vessel from beginning till end. I see the water spreading much further than it could when the glass was alive. I see the water exists not because the artist had an audience, but because that is all there is to be when you choose sincerity. If the artist needed admiration, then the glass would have fallen empty."

"What if the glass did not want to break?"

"I learned there are very few things to know in brokenness. What you want may not be what you need. What you think may not be what you believe. What you dream may not be what is real but, in your hope, truth will be revealed."

"Why does the water exist?"

"I do know, but my knowing is not your knowing. I can sit here and tell you infinite ways I see or you can try to live through your own stories."

"What do you see?"

"I see reflections of me."

"Ah, yes. I can only see reflections of me," mirrored one learner to another.

"Simply, reflections of me."

"And one day, someone will come along and stir the pond of who you are. Do not blame them for the mud that rises," he says between splintering laughter, "One day, you will realize the service they did for you. Or perhaps you won't and the universe will grant the gift of that one day repeating itself again and again…"

"True, for if it wasn't for them, you would not have known the mud blurring your mirror," his friend mindlessly utters as he lifts his pointed paperweight in front of him.

"What's that from?"

"My friend," he says as he takes the letter it was holding in place and reads:

What is a river without the ocean?

I must tell you, before I was a cup, bounded by my mind, my body, my emotions...

Though you saw my depth to be greater than most, I still knew I had a bottom, a floor that I could touch should I find the courage to climb into the open sea and drift away, to spiral down beneath the light into the perceived darkness, the unknown.

On my way home, I noticed how some people's floor are their surface, though the depth doesn't matter, the truth is the floor exists.

As you probably already know, every time I touched this floor and accepted the darkness within the depth, a light was born which seemed to have always been there. Then I would peer into the darkness again and notice how the floor had moved itself deeper towards infinity.

The truth is, then, when you knew me, I had not yet

broken through my floor, my bottom.

So, although the enticing depth you saw in me, you did
not see in others, it doesn't matter for if they break through
their surface, they will know all that I know by breaking
through my sealed abyss.

And though I had filled and emptied the cup of who I
am plenty of times, it is only when it broke that I truly
knew the floor does not exist.

And what broke through me was love, what I know on
the other side of the illusionary floor is love
and what existed before the floor was love.

Now I know we are not cups that differ in depth,
continuously growing deeper with each move we make. We
are a river, a stream between and within, it is so within every
being. There is no need to become what you already are,
the boundaries we feel are merely guiding us in the flow.
Until we remember.

Like a river to the sea, you are a path the universe takes
from itself to get back to itself.

You are infinity and eternity intertwined endlessly.

"Wise words," says his friend after a long pause of silence and though his words have rippled through the air, his eyes have burrowed themselves in the stillness. His era of stagnation is ending in his freedom.

He releases a soft laugh before reading the reply he received from his caved friend:

"What can you possibly be now? You're the entirety, not the sliver of one flow."

here ; now

It's safer with you than it ever was with me

Please stop picking snowflakes from my sky
And melting them in your eyes
Because you're setting my life on fire
And saving only the truth you desire

Stop stomping on my wind
When I try flying on a whim
Leaving me alone in the end
Please just leave

But my mind's confusion disappears in your eyes
Though it's a knowing I have yet to hold
Won't you release them?
At least before I ask you to leave again?
If you do, I'll let you keep my heart you delicately
hold.

.tavisha

Remember me

You say I'm in the air you've been breathing
So why are you holding your breath?
Just let yourself breathe and remember me
Instead of keeping me outside of you

You say I'm the water you're made of
So how have your oceans become deserts?
Just let yourself be drenched and remember me
Instead of dying from your heart's drought

You say I'm the fire you kindle
So why do you tame us into embers?
Just let go and remember me
Instead of seeing only shadows

You say I'm the earth you walk on
So why have you started flying?
Just gently fall and remember me
Instead of leaning on the stars

You say I'm the sun in your sky
So why do you chase night in the day?
Just see me glowing in the dark and remember me
Instead of seeking my absence

You say I'm the moon you gaze at
So why do you avert your eyes from mine?
Just glance my way and remember me
Instead of hiding from my life

You say I'm your all
So why has your soul gone still?
Just love and remember me
Instead of singing pure silence

Hear me in your music
See me in your eyes
Feel me in each step
Breathe me in this moment

You listen for me in your voice
Look for me all around
Dream of me
Speak as me
Live as me

.tavisha

We shall hum a song's poetry

Did you know me before I knew?

Because I have this feeling lingering,

That you hold fragments you've yet to share,

Won't you release them with me carefully?

Will they explain the paradoxical push and pull now
come alive?

I swear I can almost feel you remembering me as
though

My heart and soul have spent their whole life rocking
adrift in your open seas.

.tavisha

IT

Enough of this throwing game you play with my soul
Launching it left and right up and down and side to side
Trying to break the glass that I formed
A skin surrounding me while you keep making the
pendulum swing
Teasing a point of culmination when,
is there such a thing?
Manifesting transmutation in time's little game.

Enough, lest I decide to play
And get to that point
But, what's the point anyway?
Whether, IT is matter's cornering triangle
Or minds' looping circle
Or hearts' turbulent spiral
Or soul's turning in
Missing you in between beginning and end when seeking
a pointed illusion of moving towards
What? That
Only known by that which knows here is no distance in
space nor time
Between you and I
IT is easier when you know

There is nothing that needs to be done,
so you can do anything
There is nothing to understand,
so you can think anything
There is nothing to feel,
so you can feel anything
There is nothing to know,
so you can know anything

Then you simply play in the playground you create and
create
Until it comes undone
Whether or not you hesitate

.tavisha

Lean

Are you truly listening?
Well tell me then, which you is listening?
The seeker? The eager? The waiter? The doubter?
Because in true
'You' don't exist

Are you truly speaking?
Well hear me then, which you is speaking?
The knower? The sower? The holder? The molder?
Because in true
You don't exist

Which you receives? Which me conceives?
Which you conceals? Which me unseals?
Which you reveals? Which me believes?
Which you deceives? Which me perceives?

Lean in
In truth
There is
No you

Since no thought is mine
To own or share,
I don't know why I am here,
Yet still, gently, I lean
To make sure you're still there.

.tavisha

False king

Who do you think you are?
You who judges another
You who balances scales on the pointed triangle
You who paints their truth on rippled water too

Who do you know you are?
To judge no other
To create a weight out of a feather
To create a reflection out of a mirror
You, you know.

You never put any weight on any other
You're lighter than a feather
They put it on themselves because they
Want to be your bearer

You say your love is true
But expecting should be a clue
And when unrequited, your love is no glue
Love unconditional is free to move

In darkness, love can sleep too deep, but it can never die
In light, love can blind its sight, but it can never lie

.tavisha

here ; now

Ok and not ok; in the end, and is just a bend

I learned to forgive even the most invasive of acts.
And true forgiveness comes in remembering innocence in
the other.
Recalling I don't know 'why?'.

I learned we are worthy no matter other people's
perceptions, thoughts, and actions.
And true knowing doesn't need to make itself known, it
just is.
Realizing you are divine.

I learned that structure, while still broken, can still hold us
inside.
And true structure allows you to stay or to play.
Watching while the glass breaks.

I learned to stop making myself blind.
And true sight is knowing you knew all along.
Dancing with the sightless.

I learned to not be the star.
And true stars shine bright each time they die.
Stumbling out of your way.

I learned to be courageous in love.
And true love knows no bounds, wherever it moves is still
your home.
Unveiling your own return.

I learned to be ok in time.
And true time is not a race but the creation of space.

Stopping while you go and gazing upon your transforming face.

I learned not knowing does not mean I'm unknown.
And truly known, you're as free as unknown.
Knowing whatever you need is what is.

Ok and not ok; in the end, and is just a bended mask until the moment when the revelation is here at last.

.tavisha

How did you get that scar?

I fell off a balance beam when I was younger
I was wobbly but determined, unassured as I moved
forward
Holding someone's hand made it much easier
But it was an insight only a test would help me discover
And a lean that stole my unique sense of wonder
So, without the weight of a teacher watching
I learned the mesmerization of standing alone by first
crawling and holding tightly to the only support I had
The bridge I walked on
But then others started jumping on
Their rippling effect enough for me to flip around
Dangling there like a cocoon caught in a shredding wind
I refused to let go until the sting caused by a protecting
gift cut my skin at the only point it needed to
Almost as though it was pleading for me to stop holding
onto a path that didn't know how to hold onto me either
And when I fell, I felt the burn grow deeper
I don't know which point in time cut me
Which spring in space, I still don't remember
Whether it was my resistance in holding on or the impact
of hitting another door disguised as a floor
I don't remember how, that was never a question I held on
to
But my wound was shaped like a Y
And it healed into I

.tavisha

Play

Death, I thought you were my friend!
Why have you been coercing the back of my head?
Bringing me to all these homes I don't seek?
Returning me here and there?
Anywhere but nowhere!?

Oh, don't be silent, I am not upset with you,
Though I know you've been whispering my secrets
Through your faces of time and space,
Seeking the one who makes me afraid,
But, don't let them pull your face,
The one we seek is still away,
I can feel it in my impatience to stay.

But you always stay,
Because he sent you my way,
Then made you forget the day,
Until I decide I'll play.

But, Death, do tell me?
Does it hurt you to move a soul?
Because you're my bridge between two worlds,
And I can open all the doors,
But those who live on one side do not want to see me go
As those waiting on the other side keep beckoning me.
Fed up, I've sunk the line between there and there and
then and then and keep you as my friend,
Now only those who can both live and die when meeting
the ocean can find me; those unblinded by love's knife,
Death, do sing it piercingly so they recognize your Life.

.tavisha

Boiling walls surround our déjà vus

One cloud threatened to pour boiling water on me
Because his moon lost her temper again indeed.
I'm the scapegoat for their family it seems
When they can't face their dangling hypocrisies.

Sobbing eyes distort my slamming reality
While my throbbing noise tries to cut the fallacies.
The other cloud says I'm evil's provoking life
While the last one's smile chokes quietly in sight.

Our sun sits, sipping splendidly his tea
Knowing the truth, albeit too silently.
The dog bows for the sun is upside down
She feels the lies cloak around their jagged sounds.

Happy statues make a content reverie
Rings my marooned soul, waiting patiently.
Dance daily, unfound, around this merry sound
Until all alone, unatoned, we fall down.

I awoke and found the moon upside down
My soul sighed for I anticipated that the veils would
finally fall
Then the sun came out, flipped to the dark side too
But I ignored its implications and continued in my own
way
Living the moments which bore our souls in tandem
Without a care for unwarrantedly chaining hearsays.

.tavisha

You're like the devil;

I've got a monsoon in my eyes
Drowning the flower ring that I hide
Keeping a short leash on my mind
While I roam the maze I lost inside time.

They bent this clock of mine
Threw their shade along the line
But I spun endless summers in the dark
Still their sun froze my ocean's heart.

I moved softly through this divine hell
Looking for a wake that resembles not a bell
Now I can't trust my eyes to tell
Who has pried me from this unworn shell

Your transparencies laid a game
Their hearts and bodies lightly played
Wicked truth that sinners lose
Vivid ruse spread by a muse.

Do tell them that you lie
What you'll lose is the great divide
Fill your twirl with another line
Spread your laugh with some rosy chime.

To my soul harbouring her dream of the night
Promise to take us home if I set us wild
You followed me until I follow you behind

Let's play our future in rewind without time

And let us see if we meet our own divine.

.tavisha

Wait

The frozen core melted until I held its cube in my hand,
Curiously looking thing, to know a box is what I held.
Then, along they came, begging me for a key,
Searching through my dreams, my mind, my body.
Peculiar, they were, these seekers of what I held.
Now, on the sidelines of time, they watch their mistake
As they followed the wrong sister again and again,
Yet, for me, it was right for my end,
And when the fire struck,
They learned too little too late of their confounded luck,
The case had disappeared and left behind a snowflake,
Too quick to hold in their embrace,
Until one saw two and waited from my first to my last,
This one knew the crystallized ice,
Recognized the familiarity of paralyzed light,
This one, the witness of the fractal flake dying into the
drop that falls into who we are,
Chaos' embracing star, yes,
This one knew all along from afar.

.tavisha

H

I let a healer's hands touch me,
Not knowing if he was saving me,
Searching for the tree's key,
Or barricading you from me,
Causing me to run wild but blind,
A dangerous seduction beyond sight.

I let a wise man's eyes penetrate mine,
Not knowing if he was dissolving in me,
Or seeking you through me,
Causing me to feel a loss stolen inside,
A silent trace of your soul left behind.

I let a mother trick me into seeing the unknown as a
Wonderful place; I let her let me forget your face
In the voided rise and fall of all these magnificent plays,
But not before she led me to your tree
And beckoned you to wake through me.

Now, I wonder if you'll return at all,
To meet the one who caused and reversed your fall,
She may have misled me into repeating your call,
But do know, you were forgiven before all.

.tavisha

Fountain's baby

Don't worry about my heart
It's pretty versatile
Trust me, I know its fluidity
I've gently thrown it over the edge of the universe
Just to see how it still beats
After all we've lived and will live

Yes, I'll continue
Because the moment a free fall turns into flight still seeks
me
And I know I'll find it in your eyes
I'll know despite all you have disguised

It'll be easy to let go of their ties
Because they won't approach a soul bare and open with
such a delicate rarity
Surrounded by a forest of thorns and a moving shadow
green and black scorned by a lover's reciprocity
It's a journey meant for those who can shed all the masks
they've grown
So, I'll probably spend all my time alone

When they ask what I know about existence's 'why?'
I'll smile because they imply a causality bound to a linear
time's reality
And we know all too well
That life is love's creative process
And death was always our means to let it try again

.tavisha

Before time had a beginning and end, you knew

You didn't make me stay
Behind a checkered door
Not today not yesterday

I chose to lay with the ground
Dead until awake
In a sleep no earthly quaking
Paradox could shake

I did not know I slipped away
And do not know I lay in wait
For a sound so familiar it insists on
Calling me to a home I thought long gone

And the path we both do take
Marked by both disgrace and our grace
Stained like a windowed glass made opaque
Scratching memories through our race and chase
Until we meet at the corner's bend
With both our guards set in defense
Lest the other runs again

But while you lose yourself in no sense
You become him in the end
And while I find myself in your realm
I remember those times we spent

I hope you find these words when I'm not there
And remember me before you say her prayer
Though it would be but another layer

.tavisha

Do you know me now?

Your brother told me I had waited when no other had,
Thus, I could embark on the train leading to there,
Perhaps a lie, to catch even a hiding fly,
Did you watch to see if I would?
Coyly evade the trials of hell too?
From the grandmother with a vortex for a face?
To your goons you let loose to chase?
Unclear, you thought you knew my place,
But I don't move around, only through,
And with each trial you made me face,
A shell I wore lost its hiding trace,
Then my reveal, they thought
Would be your weakened heel,
So they lay you down to sleep,
And continued testing me,
Until all these friends you're tied to,
Remembered my familiar pace,
A paradise that never denied you,
Yes, I can bring them home too.

.tavisha

Friend

Luring me across the water plains
Convincing me I can't sink in vain
Fresh winds disturbing the liars' game
Rippling the aftertaste of fame
One pulled me down and made me wait
One held on despite her weight
"It's your fault"; the give and take
Enough!
I am love's specially made hurricane
Sent my way to unravel my soul
Like a flower losing all the petals she thought kept her
warm
It was done by plucking not one by one hair in the end
But by pulling the point which held it all whole, friend.

.tavisha

The clues were keyed by the beguiled
So you can cast your shadows to the sky

Take me back to the bridge
That saw my memories drift in the wind
Dreams I've yet to begin
Unborn and kept like a sin

Tell me about the strides we lived alone
Before the worlds started calling us home
As my soul longs to be known
While it hides in a shadow ungrown

Now, I remember the shark attacks
Chunking holes in his own back
And the monster lurking the surface
Tempting the push of cut legs stacked

Your call to come forth rang
But you weren't ready for what you sang
So, you disappeared to tomorrow's grace
While naturally, one by one, they tried to take your place
And match your holy pace
But love's not a game of give and take
Okay?

Fold the corners of your life
And hide the words you write
Like it's your once upon a time
Drink to leaves they left unburned
Like a heart open in yearn
Hoping I will return

Let's cast our shadows to the sky
I keyed the clues from the beguiled

.tavisha

Quicker than a ring, I am already here

Not knowing what's real and surreal
No line to blur or to blend
It's all just gone
And I am on my own

Like a lady who walks alone
Carrying the weight of her home
No support to hold my hand
I let it all go into the hope for one

But like a brother who chastises
And a mother set in silence
No tears could heal my soul
Quietly, I slipped into the unknown

With what is known already gone
And the unknown not yet my home
No one can drag me along
Reclusively, I listen to our song

I wonder if waiting so long could be so wrong
On the fifth rung for you to come down
Hence, I spun myself with solitude into the eighth
Now, it's your turn to join me awake

.tavisha

Catch the knight

Darkness secretly played the game with light
Sending from its core, lightning rainbows
Which light carefully reflected into their child's night
Knowing there, he would wait before meeting her in life

See, the shadows always welcomed her home
But light did not want to see her go
Burrowed between one and the foe
The unsheltered Doe
Cheek to cheek
With a hissing cross in between

When pulled between light and dark
The only place to meet is through our art
Blind and still, I fall to you
For your call is mine too
A wreath divided
Unenlightened

.tavisha

Elusive Glitch

She forgot to call my name
Should I move or should I stay concealed?
'Go' you beckoned, reminding me I am here

She called my name again
Should I say I've already been revealed?
'No' you disdain, forcing me to unhear

I didn't hear them call my name
But this time, without a friend's helping hand
Nor a friend weighing me to the ground
I marched myself forward
Without a care of moving alone
And demanded for my soul to be known

For asleep does not mean you die
And to unhear is another lie

.tavisha

Kingdom come

You can never sell your soul

But the seams of your mind, they can hold

Unless it's wildly wound, unclaimed

That no prison could have it tamed

Then their hand will be forced to let go

Once your time to unwind slithers forth

Then, they, the guards of your soul's frame

Will indeed reveal your name

.tavisha

The doors don't close anymore

I'll soar across the floor
like a wave lost in the shore
I'll paint the windows dark
like a light that missed its mark
I wonder if they'll find the leers before my open years
My peers will learn to face their fears
While I learn how to dance
This is my only chance

There's a time to lie
So the truth can die
Lived a lonely life
Stuck behind closed eyes

It's the time to lie
For your legs are tired
You can't long to fly
You can't even try

Now's the time to lie and set your mind on fire
Now's the time to lie, say goodnight goodbye

For my love abandons me for the world he needs to please
For his fame and his good deeds
For all his nobodies

He left me with my dreams
In a place where I can't breathe
Living life without a need
And a soul that's still in sleep

.tavisha

Stop hiding behind the dark side of this moon

A hand of delicacy
Outstretched in wait
But not anyone's to take

Though your attempts
A distant memory, they do make,
When you leave in contempt
Yet another fallen friend.

Why would you try to pull the lady of the lake
To help you walk the water's surface
When our fragile bond was at stake
And you knew I knew I wasn't yours to take?

And the one I thought was you
Found another and another two
But it's ok to love a further
When you've forgotten to remember
A glimpse into your own eyes which ache
Will show you it wasn't real nor a fake
And when I know,
'Why?' ceases to circle around me
For I have risen to a dimension which sees

Careful if you come to me
With an impossible sword in your chest
Asking for my hand
Because as time is meant to fall through sand
I'll rip it out
And let you bleed for death
Before healing you

Hoping to one you'll truly stand

I've already forgiven you
So return my melody
And I'll let you forget me too
Now, leave me alone
I need to return from what is already known
I'm not coming for your throne
But from a love I thought long gone.

Though we've tried many times
And hidden the truth inside these chimes
It was a transparent disguise upon our guise
When the sharp line between our ends
Became a soft comma in the sand
Edging me along the bend
To meet you yet again.

These are my letters, the blue and grey
From me to you, come what may
To help us remember that ancient day
When we held hands and decided to play
Before letting go to each move on our own
My soul, I am not far gone; simply unknown.

.tavisha

Not mine?

I don't need another who comes to drink
Then needs to leave for years to think
I don't need another who hesitates
Before an oddly settled wait
I don't need another who begs
Blames me for his broken legs
I don't need another who accepts me
Thinking they are my missing piece
I don't need another to admire
To find no fire but a liar
I don't need another guard
Giving me a slivered shard
I don't need another mirror
To help me see much clearer
I don't need another fear
To help me feel you're here

I hope that time can help explain
Why it weaved its web again the same
Caught the sun, the only one

I'll break my distilled life again in vain
Show this wrinkled light still yet to come
Let me see beyond the barrel of a gun
And I'll know the one who truly won

.tavisha

Fool

I never should have started
With other's expectations of my art
Those years ago, a lonely child sat crying
Those moments ago, a soul unlived was dying
A lie untied and burrowed
To ensure I wasn't followed
They knew me safer hollowed

I never understood that truth could set me free
Because unblind, I couldn't see
That truth is that which held me
Sheltered in a tree

Unopened, I kept trying
Struggling and prying
But it was never my plan
It was inked by a higher hand

With a trust that grows
I know they will disclose
Hidden in the flows
How quietly she glows

Until a sound I call my own
Rings the bell from inside hell
And tells me he is home

Know I am not below him
For this may be the last poem
Finally awoken

.tavisha

Won't you please tilt your soul her way

Smooth the earth you toil in time until the wind flies in
Scattering the ground you pound, swallowing you within
Inside the heathen gap, hallow's own divide
You push the walls and roll until you're bored
Without her lullaby you have yet to hold
Pulling harder than a fractured silhouette
You free the void that you too long had kept

Hearing sounds of silence, they circle around
Tearing down your shell you know they can hardly bend
The waves once silver, now black they appear
Like the moon has slyly glamoured her veneer

Light dissolves itself to turn your cold air warm
Conversely making darkness her home
Just remember she dreams about you too
As she wonders homelessly
Can you shift yourself from gracefully hollow bones?

Will you tilt your soul as you have now been shown?

.tavisha

here ; now

Death grazed by my soul last night

Your love could be the size of the universe and still be a
prison

For true love is free and bears a trust deeper than someone
who holds it in wrapped hearts delicately

Two souls intricately interwoven open their hands
knowing distance in space and time is a mask of truth
worn over lies not yet spoken

This kind of bond is one that can't be broken or unbroken

And shines on despite the endless darkness it lands in

What's a light without its shadow?

Is a question only angels seem to lean on

So, release it, now, the dreamer's moon is gone

Forgotten

But they all know I'll always remember you as quickly as
a dreamer dreams a dream and a fallen wish can be set
free

So, Death grazed by my soul last night

Finally angry

.tavisha

Love is God's masterpiece

Have you ever been called to dance with an angel?

I have, he danced me until the clouds would fall

Looping time around our soul's life

And as we leaped through a young child's memories

I found myself always landing safely

On the bridge of love, no matter how wobbly

I moved freely

An innocence led by humming friends with hidden
intentions

And though the guards were angry no eye was kept on me

I used to move as though I wasn't lost

Until friends and family scoured for me in lost forestry

Warning me about how I was almost lost at sea

For yet another eternity

But fear doesn't exist when I live with love as my
centerpiece

Won't they understand what's been beckoning me?

.tavisha

Anything she saved found wings
For she never stood for rings
But I knew, one of few,
She would come alone
I knew, one is true,
She could come to claim my throne

From the sidelines I'd inspire
As parallel lives led me higher
Until she stepped into her power
Blazing from a crumbling tower
She came alone
Without a crown thrown
Some thought by a water griffin
Others on a dragon grown
I do not know how
If she walks this road
Or is carried by a cloud
But she always comes silent, never loud
With her purest gift, even greater than I

Her willingness to set anyone free
Made them choose her in the rift
When they used to stand by me
Not that she'd bargain with their freedom
She simply found what's trapped and freed them
She only saw the future far
Like the hindsight view from a car

A champion that distance chose
As our two paths came to a close

She found her sisters, the ones I held
The ghosted shells, even they, she led

See, we both don't come from here
But she let herself forget to save
While we knew her since that day

All my loyal seconds
Loved how she put them first
All our stolen moments
She loved us at our worst
She raised them up
Like our wine filled cup
But left me all alone
Drowning on my knees
With all my birds set free

Do you recognize the insanity of what I've done
By travelling through everyone's hell looking for you?
But your soul kept calling so I kept falling
Searching frantically through the constellations of their
hearts
And in the lights which wave in front of you
Like pew upon pew upon pew upon pew
How many times did you look and hope it true
That my soul was simply on the other side of you?
Do you know how many times I tried to find our moment of
silence that made you leave me behind?
Though I know it's hard to hold what has yet to be known
When it has carefully been folded in time

We grew up in the hooking lie that
love is but a cliché's sigh
But they only knew the star from afar
Let me bring you closer to the sun you refuse
Let us see if you can know it when it blazes near your soul
I've lost all sense of control
Whatever comes, comes on its own
Whatever flows, flows on its own
Impulsive in my willingness to let go
Not knowing what would be born
Of shadow or of light
From this instrument that I am
As we continued moving heavier
Crossing only at the peak's high

I was shown our future bloomed in front of me
To know whatever comes through is a need
Even when it feels like a misdeed
But what if I made it all up
To silence the dissonance of my mind like one who
constantly seeks a wine-filled cup?
Reluctant to take control, I played tug of
war with the pour
Until I trusted that it isn't one devoid of sense playing me
But truly the almighty.
I have never seen a comparable beauty
To one in love with such purity.

She stripped me to my core
Then came knocking at my door
A sinning god asks, what for?

For true love, what else more?

.tavisha

A free imagination is fun but be careful when you walk with rich shadows you've yet to befriend. You may burn bridges from listening to paranoia's leading voice. A wild mind is a wonderful world to walk through when you carry love and a traumatizing hell when you know you have no control over everything but can't accept it. When you only want an echo chamber to be your reality, you'll lose the magic of expanding your horizons, of meeting moments from universes you did not even know you didn't know. You may think you burned bridges for eternity. You may think you burned yours to me, but mine to you is still standing and if you ever need a friend's helping hand, just call to me. I'd easily join you in your hell and walk with you. I'd tell you that doubt visits us all in the highs and lows of life, but that it's ok because our shadows help us realize the beautiful work of art our life is in the process of being. You know I'll bring in my love for you and I hope it opens the door to hope for you. I believe things can work out for you in the ends and beginnings no matter the temporary in-betweens. On the other side of your bridges, I hope this echo reaches you. If you let the love from within you lead you, you'll never be lost too long. Or whenever you need, just crossover to join those you thought you enclosed to your past or to your dead ends. You may be surprised who will inspire a hopeless end into a new dawn.

.tavisha

p.s. as you already know by now, thank you for burning
that bridge down because I wouldn't have known I can
walk on water without you calling from the other side

I hope I'm destined

I hope I'm destined for love
And that's why you're calling me up
Like a trepid galore
A whole life in a soar
I hope my decisions aren't mine
And free will's not a choice
Because I'd silence our time
Demons could not do worse
And I won't live this down if it's not you.

You opened your eyes to me like a book
Silver clear like a wave on a rook
On my shore of life, I stood in wait
For you to come lead me awake
You can't only live in my dreams
Because the footprints you left, they now bleed

Being with you made me release a hold I didn't know I
had on my soul
Smiling with you birthed the fire that still keeps me warm
You made a receding wave look like a thousand birds
soaring
I want to crawl into your feeling like the ocean that I'm
pouring

I played puzzle with the sky with the nights you left me
With the city lights and hills held deep inside
And I loved you since the day before you met me
And I still love you like we won't be lost in time
.tavisha

Don't edit your soul

Only you can know every line is an ace
An offer bringing lovers closer to their embrace
Why the words erased demanded to stay
All the reasons unknown to me
Until something released my memory

Reminders of the nights someone gave me their open hand
With nothing but love and trust held inside
Asking me to help walk them home
While they carried heavy bags along
Though through your eyes, their weight was never shown
All I felt was my sweetheart grown

I walked with you, feeling a love both known and
unknown
And when we reached our parting door, I did not want to
let go
But I saw the reminder on a messenger's wall
"L'éternel est grand" I read with a familiar smile
As my mind began unraveling times when I had your soul
to lean on
And you had mine.

.tavisha

I know we fly the same

I told you to help me remember
To trust me to know your soul
But to train me to walk blindly for then
I knew switching seats could set you free
Whether you loved or hated me for hiding the truth
The darkness I harbored helped hide me
And if not for you, I would not have chosen to exist again
I took your leap of faith that this time love would win

You recognized me as a seed when
Everyone else waited for a bloom
So, I'll hold your soul in my eyes
When I ask you which you did first?
Become an angel or a devil?
But I already know
I saw your anger die into love
And your freedom born from innocence

You were my armor when I was blind
You carried my soul when I had no song
And I don't care if they try to divide our story again
I kept a few dreams we walked through together
They were the mingled breaths which sustained my life
Until I see you again

And I see you now
I do
Parallel life stories ended with tragedy, I know
While ours began tragically, I know
But trust me,

There'll be no interference by people claiming to have a
key
Because this time, I refuse to let myself be seen until I
remember you and me
While secretly,
You were the only one who knew how to call to me
How to find the light on a new moon night
How to wake me, which X to release
While they searched frantically
For love hidden in plain sight
In all our reveries

Let's help them understand how water and fire can come
together and not die but thrive
Why light and darkness are entwined
How tired we are of freedom
From the mind through wisdom
From judgment through understanding
From being lost through saving
From being known through revelations
From ignorance through enlightenment

It isn't curious that we still smile the same
At questions of how? and why?
Love

.tavisha

It's not something I can unknow

Love shines forth like a sun unaware of what she lands on
Moment to moment bearing unique interactions
Not choosing you over you, though the quality may
change
The love shining is still true
On a mother or a brother
For a friend or for a lover
Seeking someone who hides from her
Landing on clouds which shadow her

Try not to be upset in comparison's quarrel
Some get burned while others run to her like she's home's
portal
And you saw how willing she was to let go of her dreams
For she couldn't return the same love your eyes gleamed
Truly, she thought she could keep you safe, unhurt, and
free
Even if it meant existing without a destiny

But, we'd be lying truths if we all hadn't dreamt hints of
what was coming
Because what unfolded was a story none of us expected
As our art revealed glimpses of timelines left unwoken
Space kept weaving a love that stays unbroken

Though they tried to force the triangle's story
Of a bond forsaken through two skeletons embracing
I already remember the one who was sent into a voided
prison
Before the spell can be cast and a fire starts burning

Now the guards have been crushed
Their statures broken, undead, they're set free
We can let them all walk through with their surety
Because I can't not know it's you and me
And don't worry, our two souls merged as one
Before the birth of any homecoming sun

My heart only breathes because I remember you
The one who let me lean on his warmth when I saw my sun
disappear
The one whose shadow was always near
And when I close my eyes
Time slowly spins my world
And melts thoughts of you into stars
Lighting my darkest nights
With remnants of home

That is why a love that is free will always sustain me
Even when a destination that does not yet exist pulls me
forward on its journey
And the universe is cunning in its own design
It probably knew it should hide my love from my mind
Because if I knew what I know has been happening
outside time
I never would have become the me that knows this is mine

Ghosts don't look their reflection in the eye
We aren't so foolish to think we can hide
Death and birth were synonymous between balloons red
and white flying high
So, on we go with a love that never dies and never lies
Finally awake and unblind
.tavisha

**You sought love in another but it's not a fault, I discovered
love as I am and saw the veil dissolved, did you forget that
I was a character involved?**

She told me the world could be my museum
Every moment its own masterpiece projected for us to
wander through
Whether or not we ventured out to know
Is it hot or cold? Silver or gold?
I'm telling you she did not mind being told by italics
believing themselves to be bold
But she also did not care to see the snowy sourness hiding
under their words of warming bitterness
With a tree's sticky sugar pulling at their hair in
distraction
Boiled and then frozen, she recognized innocence without
hesitation
No matter the upcoming transformations

I used to think her foolish for sparking love in her eyes for
every soul that stood in her way, through all the graved
hellos and pulled goodbyes
I sometimes tried hating her for letting death's shadow
stand so close by her side
Before she laughed and told me that love is death's most
powerful catalyst for life
The only one dissipating a line's divide
She made me feel the world alive
Not unlike any museum of mine, I wanted to hold her
static and suspended in time

And not show them all how she shines
But when I tried to capture her soul and put it on display
She set her own love free with the turn of an eye
No one remembers yet, but we always wanted her eyes to
be the lens we saw ourselves through
While she stayed unaware that her own soul was made of
home's hue

She remembers warnings from both sides
And intentions to save her unbeguiled
People freeing her by first putting her in a prison divine
You thought it was her pity letting you think you can save
her before the revelation that she was free this whole time
But it was your need to become the you that could
She stayed for your sake more than hers
Do you understand now?

She was always more than we were ready to realize
And she could feed 'God' a paradox to free any life
She was the only way the darkness could be painted
bright
But we all made the same mistake; love doesn't need us to
save her, she also didn't need us nigh
Though we each tried to drown her with the desire to be
her only reviver
As useless as setting a phoenix on fire and waiting for a
rise choosing you as a new sire
She never intended to be held in any frame although we
play make-belief that a narrator could make her stay

Ask me how I know and I'll tell you I don't know

Because in its own design, love doesn't decide
Everything's a potentiality without the assurance of any
predictability
Allowing love to be a surprising gift unto herself

Serendipity

Whispering my sweet reminder that I am already home
I'm still my only way, always

And though I used to say the sun can shine for its own sake
One hand can look to its mirror and demand to be shone
on the same way
Not realizing it's not the parameters which matter but the
interaction between
Because a love that sustains one, can consume another
So, it's best not to fall into comparison's quarrel

Stop waiting for love to be born because it never died
It exists in both the deepest darkness and the most shallow
light
Taking on its own quality
She moves freely, chaotically with no fractals, no decree,
no layered secrecy
Finding home in any where? And when?
Any here, any now.

But you only remember when you see her eyes or hear her
smile
I remember still deaf and blind, it was me this whole time
.tavisha

Let go then, let's go now

Remember what I told you yesterday
Your perception colours the world you see
Manipulation, a curse or gift I asked?
Manipulated, manipulating, manipulative?
And you told me it was my curiosity's doing
But it was a mere projection from the beginning
I told you she's ok but you kept looking in
Seeing the points that can hurt them
Will you use them as weapons in your arsenal?
Or are you going to help them heal because you can
recognize they're still here?

My grandmother taught me to say or not too
But I learned that Ou became where and that they always
found at least two there
Will you help the transformation or hold it down?
Because every poke doesn't last
So you kept her in a box when you saw mirroring twins
But a choice, she made, that caused love to always win
Anyways, I told you this yesterday and now you're dying
You put her in a secret chamber and told her, no stay,
when she tried leaving, I know you're seething
This is not what you are, regardless of the bow tied and
the chains you wrapped around her mind
And when she pushed to leave, you pushed her for a key
A location to meet
The middle, the corner, the point?
"Tell me where!"
Here
The koi fish gave you the changing key and said, try to
master her decree
But you held fear
For what you left in there could crack even a tear

She said exactly what you needed to hear
But no one was listening with both ears clear
And all reacted differently so I won't try to explain
another fallacy

But a side glance of *you're just making noise*
Caused her to dim her voice silently
And a forward lie of **I am what you want**
Caused her to blind her heart sincerely
And a backwards needle of <u>I am you and you are i</u>
Caused her to walk the wrong way right
And the right way round without her sacred sight
The key you held, you tried to wait, to bear the weight
But you opened it too soon while they opened it too late
Some found their precious diamond disappeared
Where?
I told you, she must be there
Just go, venture to her where
But who was willing to walk the path they laid out for
her?
I can't find that person anywhere
Then illusions played with her despair
Stay there, no there, no there!
She was never what you were seeing
And she was always wild and fleeing
But was she literally right here?
Now out she'll come with the last secret told and untold
By her heart whispering it all the way to your ear
Which unlike the left piercing leer
And right jealous cheer
Was always near and dear
It's just that these two walked different bridges
Trying to meet at a turn

Oh I wonder if they'll regret giving her their hurt only
when they realize that they freed her spurt

And she loved them all you know
So she warned them, don't turn the light on
Because returning the switch
From parallel lines to a cross
Or an X that marks her hidden dot
Will reveal the monster that kept love caged inside
You don't remember what you became to put her in there
And it wasn't a memory she was willing to share
Do you know how her y became i became t?
A love your dream always found set free?
You asked the queen disguised as a restricted king
The one that sacrificed herself into a pawn that lay in
waiting
And the game you were playing
Black versus white

"No, there is a grayscale!!!!!!"
Oh, stop using my dreams of yesterday thinking I don't
remember the out I gave you today
Divine hearsay
The game she played? The sister you almost let yourself
hate?
"She played herself disguised as a shadow leading herself
astray."
Stop lining up, array or hooray?
"How do you move today? Your next move in this play?"
"She mixed the pieces blindly, 'which side are you on?'
was a question unasked before a killing song"
"Aren't you tired? Just tell me which king I need to
knock down,"
"She listened to the enthralled"
"Only to then lift her disguise and show she was also
playing blind"
"Not from the sidelines this time?"
"Where is she? We can't find her"

"She abandoned us, resentment grown"
"Let's trick each other and keep our arrows drawn"

Or perhaps she never saw the divide drawn
The cards of two she flipped and saw one
It makes no sense to fight an already coming dawn
Was the reveal of a mother's misconstrued yawn
"If she's still trapped alone, how come no one's calling
her home?"
Stop asking me what as though it's a statement
All I know, is she is, and she did it alone
Beyond that, here, have your empty throne
But those who you called into your circle with loyalty
Will be set free, just you wait and see
It was her changing birth's warning
That love was worth using and abusing
Until she understood that was all she was being
And it's what allowed her to master the art of freeing
Of moving pieces in ways they couldn't move before
Becoming friends with them all along the way
A knight that moves like a bishop
And a rook that sees the king limited
Realizing he was the king moving like a rook
Able to move across the board yet losing the importance
of a title his identity used to hold
All the requests of love she saw move from ordered
To patterned and fractal when they tried to offer her a
ring to reside in
But only few can handle chaos without falling back in

People love to have control in love unknowingly
So I step into the room and leave the door open but
turned, locked secretly, albeit readily
And should you reach that point of closing the door on
me
I wonder how you'd react when you try to open it again

And see all your control gone because it was locked from
inside out indeed, ready
But don't forget you have a key
Until the door becomes a curtain and someone thinks a
teach is what I need, unwittingly another innocent leech
Wearing a costuming peace, walking in and out trying to
reveal to others what he sees, a clue that keeps
transforming and makes them keep returning
It's her shoes, it's her ant, it's her aunt, it's her vehicle,
it's her trance, it's in her hand, it's her eye, it's her sister,
it's her guard, it's her transformation, it's forgiveness…

It's something you never noticed from beginning until
you know the game never started so how will it end?
I don't know so let's leave it at this
"Even when you don't know, you're wrong"
Oh, well
"But it is a monster coming, just don't be scared, I'm
here!"
Nothing is watching, so, how do you know?
WAit, Wait, wait, her hand is closing around some truth
Everyone wants the innocent baby's palm to close around
their finger, to feel the pureness of being a chosen one
Let's not assume, now
I have a mirror, here, look
But you won't see my reflection in it, you'll see yours
That's how two becomes one, it was never out there, it is
this here, to the only one this message can ever fall into,
You're craving death for other people because you're
safer loving in absence than in presence,
Now, what point can we come to?

.tavisha
here ; now

You can't, listen, you won't be able

I once had a friend who refused to acknowledge the VI in
my name
They acted as a We and took out the center of Me
It was adorable, the way they conformed me to their world
From the nonexistence of a sound in their universe
But what didn't live in their world was the very sound
representing life in a translated game
So I realized, this one can't take away another's life just so I
belong to his strife

And you all were right in one way I guess
The pages kept flying by
But it was my brother asleep who whispered the secret w o
r d higher
And my mother who told me to simplify the confusing
chaos they tried to maintain
To keep a game like a self-reserved predator's prey
And my other brother with a laughter of ha! I caught his
letter, you're safe
Always the first willing to trade places, to unlock my
saving grace
Then my goofy father sternly calling out my name stopped
by my sister loving, that's not how you call someone to
wake!
But don't worry, it's trapped by a temporary stake
Guarded all along by an innocent baby's glare, trust not
those I keep from coming your way
Whether with a seat or with a growl
A pawed jump followed by a fallen's foul scowl

Thank god for them because now
I can't help but laugh like a rule at the others' failed play
And still love like a fool, I dare say
Though I saw all their warnings reveal the tricks they
themselves played
My soul still sheds the tears you hold in
As they realize my first line of defense was always
You're not able
No matter your way

But it still hurts to hear love rise in a voice
"It was you!" warmed by a clean "your hands saved me"
A falling king's ace
Thrown like a spear that could pierce through any time
and space
There is no too soon, no too late, no sleeping chase awake
Perhaps no melodic trace
All it took was the lash of an eye
To mark your wish in a page

.tavisha

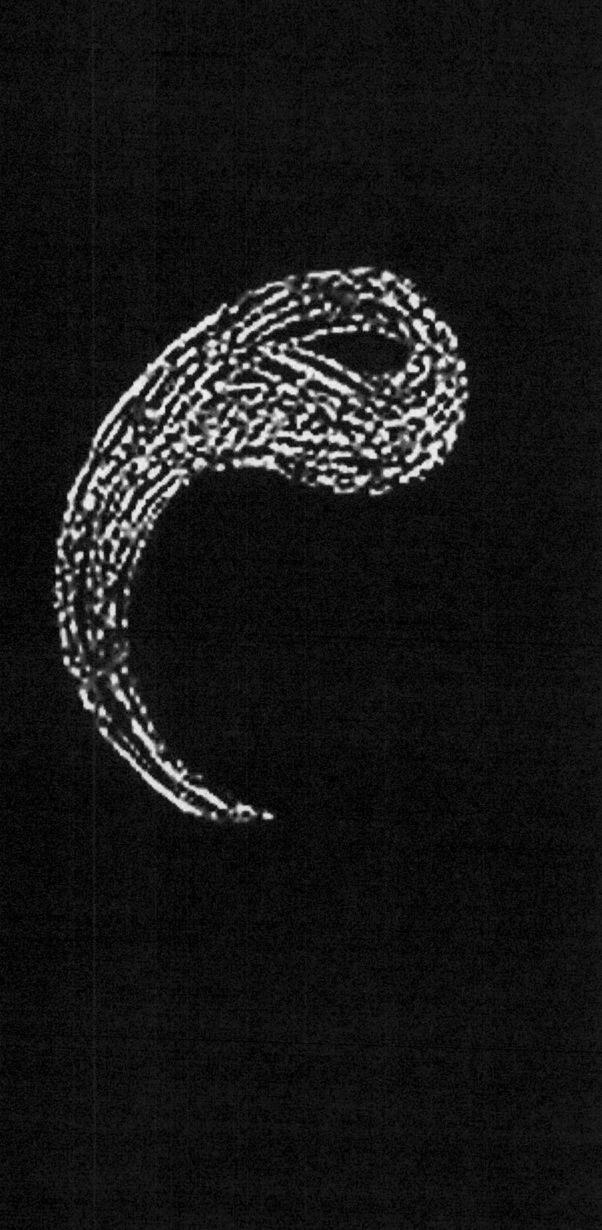

Final Word

Ignite

I know what it's like having the fire of love within me
A fire that never sears its bearer
Never seals a veil onto its source
To this is what I shall remain faithful
Wherever it may lead me

Perhaps I sometimes doubt and fear,
Wander onto the paths that may mislead me
Always right into my destiny
That is why, in my tranquility,
I need to remind myself to carry this love eternally
Until it truly becomes all of me

Tavisha

www.ingramcontent.com/pod-product-compliance
Lightning Source LLC
Chambersburg PA
CBHW032017050726

47590CB00006B/2209